*Time Travel through
the Lost Years of Jesus*

Wandering in the Mediterranean World

David Lundberg

Zante

ZANTE

Copyright © 2021 by David Lundberg
All rights reserved
Printed in the United States of America

No part of this book may be reproduced or
transmitted in any form, electronic or mechanical,
including photocopying, recording, or by any
information storage and retrieval system, without written
permission from the publisher.
For information, contact

Zante Publishing
P.O. Box 10794
Greensboro, North Carolina 27404
info@zantepub.com

ISBN: 9798707629372

Also by David Lundberg

Time Travel through Italy
Wandering with Fred and Dante

Time Travel through Ireland
Wandering through Irish Legend, Lore & More

Time Travel through Greece
Olympic Wandering

Acknowledgments

I am grateful for my upbringing as a believer in God during a stable place and time in history. I am also indebted to my wife Vasso and my friends Manar Kattan, Dr. Jerry Juhnke and Alex Vash for their helpful comments on the manuscript.

To Tolerance

A great virtue

And the foundation of even greater ones

Love

Kindness

Acceptance

<u>Tolerance</u>

Prologue

Two thousand years ago, a child was born in the Middle East. We know very little about him. He lived maybe about thirty years. The legends of his life are limited to four brief accounts known as Gospels. They each cover the last three years of his recorded earthly existence.

They are not histories. They are stories repeated in oral tradition for years until from around 70 A.D. until about 100 A.D. (roughly forty to seventy years after his crucifixion), four men in various parts of the Mediterranean world wrote different versions. It is important to realize those accounts were not written by Matthew, Mark, Luke and John. They are the Gospels *according to Matthew, Mark, Luke and John.* The first three are similar in content and style although there are variations between them. The last Gospel, *according to John*, is different in style and tone. Some of the differences have to do with the intended audience of each of the Gospels.

Two of the Gospels do mention his birth. One, *according to Matthew*, also states he and his parents fled to Egypt from Bethlehem when the child was two years old. Another Gospel, *according to Luke*, speaks of an incident when he was twelve years old and traveled with his parents to the religious capital of their world, Jerusalem.

The noted Jewish historian of the day, Josephus barely mentions this person in passing.

The Roman historian, Tacitus also speaks of him just briefly.

Jesus of Nazareth became *the most remarkable person who ever lived.* Considering his origins and how little we know of him, that is quite simply ... miraculous.

Today the majority of people on our planet either worship or revere him. Christians regard him as the Son of God. Muslims believe he was a prophet.

Popular legend views him as an illiterate peasant. This cannot be. True, there is no record of him ever writing anything on scrolls or parchment. However he was learned in the Hebrew scriptures, and he could read and write.

Jewish males of his time in Palestine were educated from the ages of five to fourteen in their synagogues. His hometown of Nazareth was tiny, just three to four hundred souls. If it had a synagogue, it was small.

As we've said, there are some accounts of his three-year earthly ministry, which began when he was about thirty years of age and ended with his crucifixion. There are also the Gnostic gospels, but they only refer to his supposed sayings. His youth and young manhood are referred to as the "lost years." No record.

Jesus of Nazareth is *the most towering figure in human history.* No one else comes close. Not the Pharaohs. Not the Caesars. No other spiritual leader or philosopher, though there have been some great ones. No Western or Eastern ruler can touch him.

What follows is a work of ***fiction***. I ask your ***tolerance***. I hope it is entertaining and enjoyable, perhaps even a bit inspiring. Let us begin.

Bethlehem

In what on our calendars is 6 B.C., a man named Joseph traveled with his betrothed wife Mary from the village of Nazareth in the Galilee region to Bethlehem in the south of Palestine. She was with child. Mary's original home was Bethlehem; her father Joachim owned flocks of sheep and goats in the region.

Soon after their arrival she gave birth to her first-born, a male child who they named Yeshua (Jesus). He was a beautiful baby and they remained in Bethlehem.

Joseph was a craftsman, a *tekton* in the Greek translation of the New Testament and he found work in Bethlehem.

Within two years noble men from far to the East arrived in Palestine. They were astrologers who had followed a blazing star, which appeared at the child's birth and led them west. Word spread of the arrival of these *magi*. Herod the Great, ruler of Palestine summoned them to his court and questioned them about this special child.

They followed the star to Bethlehem, found the *house* where Joseph and Mary lived and presented the child with gifts of gold, frankincense and myrrh. Warned in a dream, they departed secretly, not returning to Herod. Joseph also had a dream.

He said, "Mary, we must leave ... now."

"Where will we go?"

"Egypt."

"Egypt! Not Nazareth?"

"No. Herod would find the boy there. We must travel beyond his rule."

"We have no money."

Joseph said, "God always provides ... *the gifts of the magi.* I know people in Egypt. Do not be afraid. Go, pack. We leave immediately."

*****

Bethlehem today is an Arab village on the western edge of the Palestinian West Bank. Israeli settlements nearby are squeezing its borders. It is a good example of a town various political groups controlled through history and whose ethnicities (and religious affiliations) have bounced back and forth like a ping-pong ball. It's dizzying.

The town lives on tourism although there are other industries. The major attraction is the Church of the Nativity with high ceilings and a Byzantine look and feel. Today it is a Greek Orthodox place of worship. The church stands on the site of a cave, which is the traditional spot where Jesus was born. Nearby is another cave tourists (like me) visit as a facsimile of the original.

Souvenirs are plentiful in the town. I purchased an olive wood figurine of a woman carrying a jug of water on her head and one of the famous carved Bethlehem "camels."

This town is the home of David ... the shepherd-boy who became King. Since Jesus is of the royal line of David, it is natural Bethlehem is known as his birthplace.

Hebron

Joseph, Mary and the child fled the Bethlehem region. Herod sent out an edict. All children in the area of Bethlehem would be killed, *two-years old and younger*.

They traveled south to Hebron where they joined a caravan bound for Egypt. It was approximately 4 B.C.

*****

Hebron, like Bethlehem is a Palestinian city, West Bank of the Jordan River. As my tour group drove south in our bus, our Palestinian guide Matthew and his driver Raymond were great entertainment. Most of our group were in our twenties. One single, middle-aged woman, Shelley accompanied us. She was fun. We liked her.

At one point the tour bus passed an older man riding a camel, the ends of his white turban billowing backward in the wind. Raymond rolled down his window as did Shelley, seated just behind him.

"How many camels will you give us for this woman?" Raymond shouted. A huge gap-toothed grin spread across the camel-driver's wrinkled face.

"Twelve ... from Bethlehem!" Everyone in the bus broke into laughter.

We drove south through rocky countryside; many things reminded me of Bible stories. I saw flocks of goats and sheep running together and recalled how Jesus said, *"I will separate the sheep from the goats."*

To our east lay Qumran, a mountainous area on the shores of the Dead Sea. Here is where David hid when pursued by King Saul, who was afraid the young killer of Goliath would usurp him. In the Psalms, David's classic Old Testament laments of his loneliness and longing for God are heart-throbbing. This is also the area of En-Gedi, the barren stony-walled region where 3000 years after David, the Dead Sea Scrolls were discovered. I saw ruins with ancient baptismal basins where that Jewish cleansing ceremony was practiced long before John the Baptist. I gazed down at cave entrances on those bleak hillsides, dazzling sunshine lighting up sand-colored hills. At a museum in Jerusalem was a facsimile of part of those Scrolls, an almost complete replica of the Old Testament book of Isaiah. It's time-travel magic. Actually, all the Middle East is just that.

Further south on the Dead Sea erupts the majestic fortress of Masada, where forty years after the crucifixion of Jesus a magnificent and tragic saga unfolded. Before the birth of Jesus, Herod the Great built two palaces on top of this mesa-like rock formation, looking out on the Sea. Here in 73-74 A.D.

during the Jewish revolt, an extremist group took refuge and resisted Roman troops during the Roman-Jewish war. The Romans built a massive ramp of earth and stone, breeched the walls and discovered 1000 Jews had committed mass suicide rather than be taken. Only two women and three children were alive.

Our bus continued south to Hebron. The hills are sparse with large rocks strewn through the dry grass and weeds. As if God threw chunks of stone like huge, speckled gray marbles around the countryside.

Hebron is the second holiest city in Israel. Ancient ruins and artifacts. But the fascination of Hebron lies in its religious history. The Cave of the Patriarchs contains the burial sites of Abraham and Sarah, Isaac and Rebekah, Jacob and Leah. They say Rachel is buried nearby. The graves of Adam and Eve are rumored here. The place is a spiritual magnet.

It is holy to all the religions of Abraham. Judaism, Christianity and the Muslim faith. All the monotheistic (one-god) religions. There are mosques, a synagogue and a church. I marvel at how the followers of these belief systems of the one God often have such difficulty getting along.

Alexandria

The caravan Joseph and his family joined departed Hebron and crossed the Sinai, traveling west along the northern shore. The coastal road was fairly safe from bandits. The first stop was Farma in the northern Sinai. The caravan continued to Basta in eastern Egypt, then to Sakha on the west side of the Nile delta. Finally to the teeming port city of Alexandria where the family left the caravan.

Alexandria, Egypt was the second greatest city of the Roman Empire after Rome itself. Joseph had relatives here. And they had friends.

It was a Greek and Jewish city. Native Egyptians were the minority. To this day it has a European feel to it, which makes sense when you consider its journey through time. Joseph carried their meager belongings and Mary carried Yeshua. At times he walked holding his mother's hand. The Jewish quarter was directly to the left and behind the port. Joseph asked directions to his relatives' street.

Arriving at the address Joseph knocked, and a stern looking woman opened the door.

"I am Joseph of Nazareth."

A warm smile cracked across the hard face. "Joseph, we have been awaiting you! I am Miriam. Shalom!"

"Come inside! This must be Mary. Here, let me take the child! Come, Yeshua."

The small boy held out his hand. She ushered them inside.

The door closed and they were in the atrium, sunlight streaming down from the sky above, a fountain flowing in the center. Despite the heat it felt pleasant.

The lady raised her voice. "Yari, come quickly. They are here!"

Within moments a tall bearded man with salt and pepper hair appeared. His eyes glistened. He walked to Joseph and they embraced.

"I am so happy you are here, Joseph. I worried."

"We are fine, cousin. Shalom."

"Here, give me your things and I will show you to your place." Yari led them to a room in the cool rear of the house. "Rest. Joseph, I will be in the atrium." He departed.

Within minutes Joseph appeared in the courtyard. Yari reclined on cushions in Oriental fashion, the fountain gurgling happily nearby. "Please sit, Joseph. Some wine?"

Joseph sat and the two men sipped from goblets in silence. After a time Yari broke the silence. "Your son draws large attention for one so small."

The other man nodded. "Herod is unbalanced; anyone he deems a possible threat is in danger."

Yari said, "Even a two-year-old child. You are welcome here as long as you wish. I have friends and contacts. The city flourishes. There is plenty of work."

Joseph and his family stayed in Egypt three years. Herod died, but Joseph thought it best to remain in Egypt for a time. Pharos, the great lighthouse on an island in the port of Alexandria dominated the skyline.

It was 100 meters high and considered one of the Seven Wonders of the Ancient World. Built 250 years before Joseph and family arrived; it survived for another 1300 years, finally toppled by earthquakes. A man-made causeway, three-quarters of a mile long, linked the port with the lighthouse.

The marketplace of Alexandria was full of sights and smells and babbling merchants. Greek and various dialects of Aramaic were the main tongues, and after a while you could guess the merchant's origin by what he shouted at passers-by. All great fun, with the standard Mediterranean custom of haggling over prices.

The Library of Alexandria was the greatest in the Western world in antiquity. Its scholarship and prestige unsurpassed. By the time Joseph and family arrived it was starting to decline somewhat in influence. A few Greek scholars were leaving, but many Jews and others remained and continued their work. It was located directly to the left of Pharos as viewed from the sea in the center of Alexandria with the Jewish quarter slightly east.

Joseph found work among the Greek and Hebrew builders. Mary tended to her child and helped Miriam around the home. Yeshua adjusted to his cousins and their friends, laughing, playing children's games. One afternoon Miriam and Mary prepared the evening meal and Miriam said, "Yeshua is a happy child." Mary nodded.

"He is also different."

Mary glanced at the other woman.

"He is not selfish; he shares easily. But he does not follow the other children. He goes his own way."

"He is not yet three years old."

"Mary, I have older children and I have watched their friends. Yeshua is not like them. He is very intelligent, but there is something else. He is what I call intuitive. He understands beyond the talking, beyond simple thinking and beneath the ... well, beneath the surface. I have not seen a child quite like this before. Tell me more about these *magi* who arrived and gave him treasures."

"They came to our house in Bethlehem and they presented rich gifts. We used those gifts to travel to Egypt. Their names were Caspar, Melchior and Balthazar. They came from the East: Arabia, Persia and India."

"Their beliefs?"

"I think they were followers of Zoroaster."

Miriam said, "I have heard of this. Those people are like us. They believe in one God, unlike the Greeks."

"I have heard this also."

After a year in Alexandria as Joseph and Yari relaxed one evening, Joseph spoke. "My dear friend and relative, I am leaving for a time. I will take Yeshua, and we will travel to Cairo and then up the Nile. I would like Mary to remain here."

"Of course Mary may stay with us. She is now part of our family. But for what reason would you take a three-year-old child on such a trip?"

"I do not know."

"You do not know! Joseph, you are a practical man but sometimes you mystify me."

"Sometimes I mystify myself, but I know I must take Yeshua on this journey."

"I need more wine," Yari said, refilling his goblet.

Within a few days Joseph was ready to depart. Mary asked, "How long will you be gone?"

"Several months at least, my dear. Do not worry. You know I will be careful."

"Of course. Shalom."

Joseph swung his camel, Yeshua clinging close behind him and they started off, south and to the east. First came Wadi Natrun then great Cairo. Then Gabal El-Tair and finally Assiut, south toward the source of the Nile.

A wadi is a ravine or river valley, sometimes dry, but in rainy season it attracts water. Date palms and shade. Dates are the nectar of the Mediterranean. Joseph and Yeshua made it to Wadi Natrun the first day, and they rested for two nights. Then on to Cairo. Joseph found a caravan city on the west edge of the city, hobbled their camel and joined the communal gathering for evening meal. Later he and the boy pitched their tent and unrolled blankets for sleep. North African nights can be very cold after the heat of day.

The next morning after tea and bread, Joseph and Yeshua set off for Cairo. They entered the western portion of the city. The boy looked up and said, "Father, I cannot see anything. There are walls of people all around." Joseph hoisted the child over his shoulders.

"How is this, Yeshua?"

"Wonderful! I see everything. I am on the camel again."

Joseph thought, *"I will not take that as an insult."*

The language mix was different than Alexandria. Little Greek or Hebrew Aramaic, more Egyptian dialects. This western side of the city showed the most development. In one of the marketplaces Joseph lowered the boy.

"Stay close, Yeshua. Here ... carry the water jug."

Joseph purchased bread, cheese and fruit. They found a shady corner near a tree, reclined and ate lunch. As they ate the child said, "Father, why do so many people live in cities?"

"I do not know. Perhaps because there is more work in cities. Then again, there are more people."

Joseph thought for a moment. "What do you think?"

"Maybe they are lonely."

The man looked at the boy for some time then laid his head on the ground near the base of the tree and fell asleep.

Joseph's eyes opened. The child sat, watching the crowds in the market. The older man rose and stretched. The sun arched across the afternoon sky, declining.

"Yeshua, let us go. Would you like to walk around the city more?"

"No, Father. I am ready to go back."

"Good. So am I."

Joseph lifted the boy on his shoulders and headed west toward the caravan site. "Child, somewhere in this area, the land of Goshen is where our great father Moses grew up. He led our people east across the desert to Palestine where you were born. I wanted you to see this."

When the crowds thinned he lifted the boy from his shoulders, and they walked side by side toward the caravan. The sun was low in the west. Joseph un-hobbled their camel so it could graze, then they joined the communal fire. They remained another day and night to rest. Early the following morning they rose before sunrise, saddled their camel and headed south.

Their destination was Gabal El-Tair on the east side of the Nile. Both of them grew dark-skinned from the blazing sun. In late afternoon a large hill rose on their left across the river. A few boats carried cargo, animals and passengers back and forth from the west bank to the east.

Disembarking from the craft on the east side, they mounted the camel and it plodded up the hill. There were a few scattered dwellings near the top. Joseph called to one of the walkers, "Is there an inn?"

The man pointed straight ahead. "There." Joseph moved on and dismounted. "Here Yeshua, hold the reins."

He knocked and pushed the door open. A man sat at a small desk.

"Yes, may I help you?"

"I am looking for a room, myself and a boy."

"We have a room."

"I have a camel."

"There is a stable in the rear."

"Very well. We are hungry. Do you have food?"

"Yes, we have a small kitchen."

They settled into their room. "Come Yeshua, we eat a real meal, enough bread and cheese."

The next day Joseph and the child explored the top of the limestone hill, riddled with small caves. The barren sand-colored, pock-marked hilltop dropped straight down onto a deep green carpet of flat farmland with the blue Nile River flowing past back to Cairo and the sea. The boy said, "Look at all the birds flying."

"This place is well known for them. Gabal El-Tair means *Mountain of Birds*.

"What are those white ones?"

"Those are storks. They migrate this time of year thousands of miles from across the sea to the north, then down the Nile River."

"What is 'migrate'?"

"Travel."

"Why do they travel?"

"I do not know. Perhaps the change of the seasons."

They stayed two days. Then they rose early, made their way to the ferry boat, crossed to the west bank and continued south toward Assiut.

For centuries Assiut (or Lycopolis in the Greek) was a place of trading and agriculture where caravans crossed. There was a small Jewish population and Joseph fell in with them, finding work as he had in Alexandria.

One night Yeshua said, "Father, how long will we stay here?"

"I do not know. Longer than the other places.

Assiut is the hottest settlement on the Nile River. They arrived in fall as things cooled a bit. One evening the child asked, "What does Lycopolis mean?"

"City of the Wolf. In the legends of this area wolves defended it in ancient times. These people revere the wolf."

"They worship an animal?"

"In a way."

One day Joseph said, "We are leaving, son. Back to Alexandria."

"Good, I miss Mother."

"So do I."

They departed the next morning, retracing the steps they took to Assiut. It took a week. After arriving in Alexandria and stabling the animal they walked to Yari and Miriam's house. Joseph said, "Child, you knock on the door."

He rapped three times. Mary opened it.

She fell to her knees, arms circling the boy. "Yeshua, I have missed you so much!" Tears ran down her cheeks. He hugged his mother and patted her on the back as she sobbed. "You are so big and dark as an Arab!" She grabbed his hand and pulled him inside.

"Miriam, Yari! They have returned!"

Miriam burst into the atrium with Yari close behind. Miriam embraced the child. "Are you hungry, ... tired?"

"Both."

She grabbed his hand and hustled them to the kitchen. Yari said, "Welcome back ... of course, we were concerned. Chilled wine?"

"Certainly."

Yari said, "I hope the wanderlust is out of you."

"Yes."

"Joseph, stay here in Alexandria. Life is good. Miriam and I love Mary and the boy ... and well ... you are all right."

Joseph burst out laughing. "Thank you."

"I mean it. Yeshua will get a fine education here. There is no unrest. You have some money left. We can find a small house. There is work."

"I will think on it. I must tell you how grateful I am for how you sheltered us. You are more than a relative. You treated me as a brother."

Yari nodded.

Some months later Joseph said, "Yari, we are leaving."

"Where now?"

"Back to Palestine."

"What! Are you crazy! There is unrest there. Stay here."

"Mary and I are homesick, and we feel Yeshua should grow up in the land of his birth."

"*If* he grows up! Remember why you came here in the first place."

"I remember."

"Where will you go?"

"To the Galilee. It is my home."

"And a hotbed of sedition. You are a stubborn man, Joseph."

"Well, they say we are a stiff-necked people."

Yari leaned back and took a sip of his wine. "I will miss you, cousin."

"Myself, also."

Within two weeks Joseph had the camels saddled. Tears ran down Miriam's cheeks. Yari looked stern.

"Remember. If things go badly you always have a home here."

Joseph said, "I know, brother. Thank you for everything."

He wheeled his camel and started east, Mary and the boy following. They took the same path across Egypt and the northern Sinai to Hebron, then Bethlehem. Arriving in the city of David, they proceeded to her parents' house. Joachaim saw them approach in late afternoon and threw down his hoe. "My child!" He ran and threw his arms around her. "Anna, Mary is here!"

Anna burst from the house and cried, "Oh, Mary!" She ran and embraced her daughter and the boy.

After a few days, when the women had retired Joachim said, "Joseph, what will you do?"

"We will go back to the Galilee, to Nazareth."

Joachim thought for a moment. "Actually it is not a bad idea. The word is they will build a new city near Nazareth, expanding the town of Sepphoris. Herod's son intends to make it his capital of the north; there will be much work in building. It suits you, Joseph. Sepphoris is less than four miles from Nazareth."

He continued. "I have thought of leaving Bethlehem. As you know, my home is Nazareth, like you. The grazing land is better in Galilee. I know the rabbis in Sepphoris. Good men, not like those scoundrels in Jerusalem. With you and Mary going it would be even more attractive. Let us talk more."

Within a week Joseph prepared to travel. Joachim and Anna made their decision. They settled their affairs in Bethlehem. Joachim acquired grazing rights for his flocks in Galilee and hired men to drive his animals north.

Joseph, Mary and Yeshua started in the morning, heading north through Judea, traveling past cities and towns whose names ring down through history. Bethany, Jericho and of course Jerusalem, the City of Peace that has seldom known peace and in less than two generations was leveled and destroyed by the Romans in retaliation for Jewish resistance. Then began the great Jewish Diaspora spreading those people throughout the Mediterranean and European worlds and much further, to the ends of the earth.

Jericho

First came Jericho, the fabled first city where Joshua led the Hebrews after Moses on their trek from Egypt; some say it is the oldest city in the world. There are still some walls as in the legends when Joshua and his people circled the city, blew their rams' horns and the walls came "tumbling down."

It was in Jericho where I came upon the most beautiful bougainvillea I have ever seen, and I love bougainvillea. Not native to the Mediterranean, it thrives here. The one I remember was the size of a tree with bright red and pure white blossoms intermingled beneath a deep blue, cloudless sky like the colors of the American flag.

Bougainvillea is my favorite plant. It is native to South America. A French explorer's botanist "discovered" it on a voyage in 1789. Legend says the botanist's lover and assistant found it. She disguised herself as a man to make the voyage. French military ships did not permit women in those times.

The botanist's name was Commercon. His French admiral was Louis Antoine de Bougainville.

The botanist's assistant became the first woman to circumnavigate the globe.

I first encountered bougainvillea when I lived in Greece in the 1970s. I fell in love with it as I did with a Greek woman and with Greece.

It does not do well in the ground in North Carolina. South Carolina to Florida, OK.

So I use pots.

To this day when I see bougainvillea in Florida, the Mediterranean, wherever, I'm still enthralled.

The color on this plant comes from the leaves, not the flowers. Therefore we have marvelous color from midsummer to fall.

Various species of bougainvillea are the official plants of Guam; several counties in Taiwan; Ipoh, Malaysia; three towns in California; five cities in China; three places in Okinawa. It is the national flower of Grenada.

Samaria

Joseph and Mary moved on. They passed Jerusalem to the west, then the town of Ramallah was on the east. It is today a Palestinian city and sits alone on a high hill as do so many Middle Eastern towns, perched up there for centuries for defensive reasons. Then they passed the region of Samaria to the west.

*****

Our tour bus continued north to Shechem/Sychar, traditional site of Jacob's Well, also known as the well where Jesus spoke to the Samaritan woman. When I visited in the 1970s, the Greek Orthodox Church above the well was incomplete, no roof. There were two passageways to the well below ground. This is the thing when visiting ancient sites. The rubble of the centuries has piled up, and the traditional area is below ground level.

I loved it. We looked up at the sky overhead; there were few tourists. I felt I had a bit of the feeling of how it was in ancient times. Time travel.

Today the Church is completed and it is lovely also. Bright and airy, well-lit and typical Orthodox style. Beautiful in a different way.

I adore the story of the Samaritan woman.

*****

Jesus and his disciples headed north to the Galilee. They stopped in Shechem, and Jesus rested by the well of Jacob while his followers did their "disciple thing." They headed to the market for food. A local woman came to the well and Jesus entered into conversation with her. He told her to call her husband and she said she had none.

Jesus replied she had spoken truthfully; she had had five husbands and the man she was now with was not her husband. The woman, obviously flabbergasted, declared Jesus must be a prophet. The disciples returned. They were amazed Jesus talked to this local woman and no one questioned his motives.

First of all, it would not be proper to speak to an unknown woman. Second, Jews had no dealings with Samaritans. The differences between these groups were slight, but isn't that the way it always is? We split hairs about our differences when we are all children of God.

The great thing for me is the magic and implied divinity in this interchange.

The other great New Testament story of this area is the "Good Samaritan." A "lawyer" asked Jesus, "Teacher, what shall I do to inherit eternal life?"

Jesus put it back on him. "You know the Scriptures. What do they say?"

The lawyer answered, "You shall love the Lord your God with all your heart, mind, soul and strength, and your neighbor as yourself."

The lawyer then asked, "Who is my neighbor?"

This was one of the constant, trick questions when religious figures tried to pin Jesus down. He then told a story of how bandits attacked a Jewish man traveling alone, who left him half-dead on the road. Two Jewish "religious authorities" passed the wounded man one after the other, ignoring him. Then a Samaritan saw him, stopped, rendered aid, took him to an inn, provided for his recovery and told the innkeeper if there were additional expenses, the Samaritan would cover it on his next visit.

Jesus' simple question to the man questioning him, "Which of the three was this man's neighbor?"

Tiberias

The two camels and the Holy Family continued north and the Sea of Galilee appeared. The town of Tiberias lies on the west coast. Within the lifetime of Jesus it grew as Herod Antipas, son of Herod the Great, made it his second northern capital after Sepphoris. It was the last stop before Nazareth.

*****

Our tour bus stopped in Tiberias for the night. Antipas named it for Tiberius, the Roman emperor who was his patron. The Romans divided Palestine between the three sons of Herod the Great and one daughter. Antipas received the more northern territories including Galilee. This region was a beehive of rebellion, and Antipas involved himself in the executions of both John the Baptist and Jesus of Nazareth.

We looked out from our hotel upon the placid Sea of Galilee. On the other side of the water rose the Golan Heights, which Israel wrested from Arab control in the twentieth century. Of great strategic importance, the Heights dominate that northeastern side of the sea. It was a spring evening; we enjoyed a fine meal at our hotel. The restaurant manager and a friend circulated around the tables. Being rather young and naive I broke into conversation with them, looked at the manager's friend and said, "Are you Jewish or Arab?" I couldn't tell.

He looked at me without blinking and said, "I'm Greek Orthodox."

His straight, assertive, confident response confirmed it for me. I could have been back in the center of Athens.

The next day we headed north to Nazareth.

Along the way we stopped for fuel; there was a roadside market across from the gas station. Raymond walked to the stall and soon munched on a huge stalk of lettuce, straight from the vendor. Matthew looked at us and said, "Raymond can eat that, he was born in this country. None of you!"

Nazareth

Joseph, Mary, the child and their two camels continued, passing Tiberias then on to Nazareth. They arrived at their home, now deserted for over five years, rundown and desolate. Joseph set to work restoring it. Within a few weeks it was respectable again.

Meanwhile, Joachim and Anna moved their flocks north, arrived in Nazareth and settled the animals in the valley to the west, looking toward Sepphoris. It was good pastureland. Joachim renewed his contacts with the rabbis of Sepphoris and looked for a house on the east edge of that town close to his flocks.

Yeshua began attending Hebrew school at the small synagogue in Nazareth. Routine settled in for the extended family. When Joseph had no work building he helped Joachim with the animals. As the scriptures indicate, Mary had more children. Yeshua acquired younger brothers and sisters. He outgrew the limited synagogue school in tiny Nazareth and began attending the school in Sepphoris, taught by rabbis. His grandfather was a faithful contributor to the synagogue.

When not schooling, Yeshua helped his grandfather with the flocks. He enjoyed it but he enjoyed most everything. He began helping Joseph with building. The construction increased in Sepphoris; he helped more and more.

Soon he spent his weeks in Sepphoris, but he went to Nazareth and his parents' home for Sabbath and the weekend.

*****

Nazareth has changed since the days of Jesus. In his time it was a tiny village of maybe 400 souls. Today the city has about 70,000 inhabitants and the metropolitan area around 200,000. Time has moved on. It has been a Palestinian place for many years.

There are Christian shrines and places of worship. Most dominant is the Church of the Annunciation rising on the hillside, its dome an inverted, dark ice cream cone with the nave below looking vanilla-like. Walls circling the sanctuary are the same light color, fringed with orange terra-cotta roofing so common in the Mediterranean world.

Nazareth never had the best reputation. When Jesus recruited his disciples, at one point Phillip went to his friend Nathaniel and told him he had found the Messiah, Jesus of Nazareth. Nathaniel replied, *"Can anything good come from Nazareth?"*

Our Palestinian guide and the bus driver told us this was one place we should beware of pickpockets. Whether it was true or not I don't know, but I was careful and came away with my wallet intact.

Sepphoris

One evening in Sepphoris Joachim and Joseph sat sipping tea by candlelight. Anna and Yeshua had retired for the night. Joachim said, "Joseph, I have some business in the Mount Carmel area. I want to take Yeshua with me."

"Why?"

"It is a holy place for our people and it is beautiful. I want Yeshua to see it."

"If you wish. You love the boy."

"Everyone loves that child."

Within a few days Joachim was ready to depart. He prepared a camel and Yeshua approached. "Here young man, you ride this animal."

"I ride my own camel?!"

"Of course, you are old enough."

Joachim prepared another mount and they set off.

They traveled west, climbing the ridge to the heights of Mount Carmel overlooking the Mediterranean Sea. Caves filled the area.

"Yeshua, this is the area where our great father, Elijah destroyed the priests of Baal. It is peaceful now."

"It is beautiful."

"Come. We must get down to the water and Ptolemais before sundown. This place is not safe at night."

Haifa

Viewed from Mount Carmel the city of Haifa is a jewel. Lush green hillsides, so uncommon in Israel, look down on a fine semicircular bay. Haifa grew from nothing in the days of Jesus to the third largest city in the Holy Land today. Palestine is the country of faiths: Jewish, Muslim, Christian. Haifa is home to the temple of the Bahai faith, an offshoot of Islam, although Iran and India have the largest populations of Bahai followers.

Looking down from Carmel the gold-domed Bahai temple dominates the slope. Nineteen large balcony-like terraces extend like porches up and down the hillside from the shrine. As if God carved huge steps down to the temple, then below it to the city. He manicured each terrace with multi-colored flowers and orange pathways mirroring the terra-cotta roofs all around Haifa. There are several blazing white Greek temples on the location, like someone lifted them in perfect condition from Sicily or Greece of 2,500 years ago. Surrounding the golden shrine are rows of tall, pointed cypress trees, the fingers of God pointing upward to the heavens.

In Israel they say, "If you want to work you go to Tel Aviv; if you want to pray you go to Jerusalem; if you want to live you go to Haifa." I don't know if the quality of life here is any better than other places in Palestine, but if I could look down every day from the summit and its Roman Catholic Carmelite monastery upon this bay, I would give Haifa my vote. I could find almost any faith I wanted.

*****

Joachim and Yeshua found an inn and spent two days in Ptolemais (now known as Acre), the main port of the region. Joachim finished his business and they started back to Sepphoris. Traveling due east, passing Tel Makor.

Tel Makor is the site of James Michener's great historical novel, "The Source." Michener wrote many fine books. "The Source" is my favorite. It weaves a story of the Tel's development through time.

The boy neared twelve years of age, his life balanced between the rabbinical schools in Sepphoris, the flocks of his grandfather, and helping Joseph in the building trade. As the Scriptures say, *"He grew in wisdom and stature, in favor with God and man."*

It was customary in those times for young Hebrew males at age twelve to travel to Jerusalem for confirmation as young men. Joseph and Mary prepared for the journey with Yeshua. The local rabbis from Sepphoris accompanied them as did other families with twelve-year-old boys. They entrusted their other children to friends in Nazareth.

The entourage set off, heading directly south. The first night they camped near Megiddo. Tel Megiddo looks out upon the Jezreel Valley, which stretches northwest to southeast from the Haifa area to the Jordan River. Megiddo is like Tel Makor, an ancient dwelling place where generations of people built a settlement that eventually fell into disuse and decay. In time another community was built on the ruins. The valley of Jezreel was the place of several ancient battles. One in which Gideon and his forces were victorious, another in which King Saul and his armies were not. The New Testament hints this is the site of the most climactic battle of human history.

Mount Megiddo. Har Megiddo. *Armageddon.*

The next day the group moved southwest through the pass in the Carmel ridge, heading for the sea. They approached Jaffa, one of the main ports on the Mediterranean, then moved south along the coast a short distance. Here they camped for the night.

Jaffa/Tel Aviv

My memories of Jaffa are of walking along the beach and seeing expensive villas gazing out upon the sea. All those homes were the color of sand; the seashore sprouting up into rich dwellings.

Tel Aviv, just north of Jaffa has exploded into prominence. After Israel gained a nation and independence in the late 1940s, many of the surging immigrants clustered in Tel Aviv. Today it is the bustling commercial center of Israel; only Jerusalem rivals it in size. The city of Jerusalem is greater; the metropolitan area of Tel Aviv is larger. After landing at the airport and being disoriented by the armed guards all sporting machine guns, we drove to our seaside hotel for the evening. Everything sparkled. Lights, vitality. Tel Aviv-Jaffa reflects nightlife and energy. If you want a gentle peaceful life, don't come here. If you want excitement, business or work, come on!

Jerusalem

The next day the caravan set off for the greatest city. No words can describe Jerusalem, and many words have tried. Viewed from any angle it is magnificent. The group from Galilee approached from the west. No matter which direction you travel, it is always "up to Jerusalem." You ascend the heights. If you come from the Mediterranean direction the climb is long, barren, uphill, then you crest the rise and there it is. Timeless and still, ... from a distance. You draw near; life begins.

The Galileans pitched their camp on the outskirts of town. Soon a fire roared and laughter surged. Food distributed and stories told. Then retold. Families retired for the night.

The next morning the rabbis gathered in the center of camp with the twelve-year-olds. "We take the boys into the city to the temple to meet with the priests. Any of you parents may come or visit the city or remain here. Your choice." All the parents followed the rabbis and children to the temple.

Old Jerusalem is a great walled city perched on a ridge, glowing in sunshine, a sprawling eagle with a great breast of green trees, looking east across the Kidron valley to the Mount of Olives. The people of Galilee circled around to the east and entered the city through the great double Golden Gate, which led directly to the Temple Mount. They entered the outside portico of the temple and other men met them.

Introductions began. The local head rabbi spoke. "Rabbis of Galilee, you and the boys come with us. Parents, you may remain here. We will interview the children and return in some time." The group departed.

The morning moved on and the temperature rose. Sweat glistened on the foreheads of mothers and fathers. Around noon the boys and men emerged. The head rabbi spoke. "Return tomorrow morning; we will speak again." They turned and left.

The parents and children departed through the eastern gate. They circled around to the north and entered the city through the great Damascus gate. Soon they were in a maelstrom, a sea of energy, sights, smells and excitement. They found the first marketplace and loaded up on vegetables, bread, cheese and a bit of dried fish. The heat of day bore down. They retreated back through the gate, on to their campsite and rested.

After the evening communal dinner Joseph, Mary, Yeshua and one of his young friends went back to their tent and fell asleep. The night was crisp and cold, but the blankets warm and they slept well.

Two more mornings they trudged to the eastern gate and left their boys for questioning by the rabbis and priests. Some of the parents departed for a time to explore more of the city. Joseph and Mary waited until the boys came back. On the third morning near noon the chief rabbi returned with the children, raised his hands and proclaimed, "These are no longer boys, they are men! They have met our expectations. Congratulations to you fine parents and you rabbis from Galilee for your good instruction!"

Parents' eyes shone and arms rose in happiness. There was singing and joy around the campfire after darkness. It went later than usual.

The Entrances to Jerusalem

The doors and gates of Jerusalem are marvelous. I have a large wall hanging in my home reflecting thirty different doors of dwellings in the city, each unique. I believe my wife bought it.

The poster reminds me of the foolishness of stereotyping and bigotry. Each of those exquisite doors varies a great deal. Some are single doors, some double. The colors change from brown to various shades of green, bronze, some silver-plated. Greek design, Arabic, Hebrew, Christian, Roman, French and all sorts of mixtures. Some doorways have deep entrances; others are flat on the street. Some ornate, others quite simple.

As I lived in different countries, I realized a certain culture does not mean people are the same. No, not at all ... it means they share a common bond. I find people in so-called "unified" cultures (like Greece or Italy or Germany) are often more distinct individuals than those in diverse cultures (like America or Canada). Somehow those in the "unified" cultures have the freedom to develop and display their unique personalities while still "belonging" to their distinct ethnicity. This is a beautiful thing.

The Gates of Jerusalem echo a similar theme of diversity. You see references to the "Eight Gates of Jerusalem" or the "Twelve Gates of Jerusalem," sometimes the "Nine." It all depends when you land in time. Today the main gates of the old city of Jerusalem are as follows.

First, the Damascus Gate on the north side of the city. Always bustling, leading to exciting marketplaces you enter a world, both ancient and modern. Below and to the left of the entrance, half buried is the former Damascus Gate, now bypassed by the higher modern one. It is a picture of time gone by, the rubble of the centuries piled up and a new gate constructed above the debris. Time travel in a snapshot.

Herod's Gate comes next, also looking north. It has nothing to do with Herod, but it was once thought Herod's palace was inside the gate. Not true, but the name stuck. This is a simple entrance leading into the Muslim quarter.

As we circle around to the east, we come to the Lion's Gate (St. Stephen's Gate). This is the traditional place where Stephen, the first Christian martyr was stoned to death. I like this gate. It has a human feel to it. Rather small, not busy, it also leads to the Muslim quarter. Carved lions to the right and left above the entrance. If there was water in the valley below I'd think I was in Venice, looking up at Venetian lions of stone. But there is no water.

Moving down the east side of the city walls, we come upon the glorious double Golden Gate, entrance to the great Temple Mount. It was once sealed to prevent the returning Messiah from entering Jerusalem through it (good luck); it gleams in the morning sunshine like a radiant challenge. Just before it lies a Christian cemetery where hopeful souls have been buried, wishing to be the first to rise when the Messiah returns.

Looking at this great, glowing gate we retreat backwards down into the Kidron Valley, then further back up onto the Mount of Olives, which holds the Garden of Gethsemane where Jesus prayed before being seized prior to his crucifixion. Some say the thick, gnarled trunks of the ancient olive trees in the garden were there when Jesus wept the night of his passion. If you want to travel back through time, visit this Garden. It's that simple ... and magical.

Circling around to the south side of the city, we come to the Dung Gate. It looks a lot better than it sounds. It's an ancient entrance from Old Testament times. In the modern era refuse was hauled out this gate, hence the name. It is the traditional area where one New Testament reference states Judas Iscariot plunged after his betrayal of Jesus, his innards bursting after he fell. Another New Testament reference says he hanged himself. Go figure.

The Dung Gate leads into the Jewish Quarter of the city and the Temple Mount. The area of the Temple Mount is holy to both Muslims and Jews. The lower portion of the Western or Wailing Wall is built of massive Herodian stones (those Herods sure did a lot of building), some as large as 12 X 4 X 3 meters and weighing as much as 600 tons. Devout Jews pray at the wall with numerous small slips of paper (prayer notes) wedged between the stones.

When I first traveled to Greece on military assignment I took a Trans World Airlines flight from New York to Athens. After the seatbelt sign went out, dark-clothed men with hats having wide brims circling their heads filed to the bulkhead, stood before it and began rocking back and forth. They were praying. I had never seen Greek Orthodox priests so I assumed that. Then I discovered the flight was going on to Tel Aviv after Athens. I had never seen Orthodox Jews either. Well, I had now. I later saw the same rocking action at the Western Wall.

Above the Wall is the Temple Mount and the Dome of the Rock; this image more than any other symbolizes Jerusalem. An eight-sided mosque built after a Byzantine church design with a white base, sky-blue mosaic-like upper walls and the magnificent golden dome crowning it. Tradition is here Abraham was to sacrifice Isaac and here Mohammed ascended to heaven. Everyone must remove their shoes before entering the mosque. I wondered if I would find mine upon exiting. No problem.

The Zion Gate, also on the south side of the walled city is unimposing. It leads to the Jewish quarter on the right and the Armenian quarter directly ahead.

Noted for pockmarks from weapons fired during the 1967 war when Israeli forces stormed through and captured the old city. Their leader was a one-eyed Jewish commander with an eye-patch (the defense minister) who symbolized Israeli military prowess, Moshe Dayan.

Continuing around, the Jaffa gate lies on the west side of the city and leads directly to the Christian quarter. It is a simple entrance, built in an L-shape for defensive purposes. It is so named because it faces west to Jaffa and the Mediterranean coast.

Finally, the New Gate on the western side leads into the Christian sector. Built "relatively" recently and busy with cars and bus traffic.

*****

Joseph and Mary crawled under their blankets.

"Joseph, Yeshua is not here."

"Do not worry; he is with a friend. Go to sleep."

The morning broke bright and clear. They saddled their camels and waited to depart with the caravan.

"Joseph, I still do not see the child."

"He is now a young man. Let him enjoy a bit of independence."

The group set off, bound for Jaffa. By evening they arrived at their former campsite.

"Mary, prepare the tent. I will get Yeshua. See you at the fire."

Mary joined the party for dinner. After some time her husband appeared with two other men. One had his hand on Joseph's shoulder. He walked to Mary.

"Yeshua is not here."

Mary leaped to her feet. "What! Where is he?"

"He must still be in Jerusalem."

"What will we do?"

"It is too late to do anything now. Tomorrow morning we return to Jerusalem. Yeshua is smart. We will find him."

"I am worried, Joseph!"

Joseph grunted, but he worried too.

"Go to sleep."

Mary did not sleep all night. Joseph only a little. At dawn they saddled their mounts and headed east toward Jerusalem, traveling hard. By mid-afternoon they reached the gates, camels groaning. They circled the walls to the Golden Gate. Joseph hobbled the animals and they rushed into the Temple portico. There they froze.

A group of rabbis sat in a circle, Yeshua seated in the middle. He was speaking to them, all the older men silent, listening. Mary burst upon the group.

"Son, why have you treated us this way? We are distressed, searching for you!"

Yeshua gazed at his mother. *"Why were you looking for me? Did you not know I must be in my Father's house?"*

Mary stared at the floor. Joseph gazed at the group and a thin smile spread across his face, remembering the time spent traveling alone with Yeshua in Egypt. "Come son, we must go."

The rabbis rose and one stepped forward. "Thank you sir, for allowing us this time with the boy."

Joseph nodded and they departed. He found an inn near the Damascus gate and they settled for the night. After a good meal and a solid night's rest they were up at dawn, loading the animals. Mary looked at her husband. "Where do we go?"

"We head north along the Jordan River then strike west up the Jezreel valley. With luck we will catch up with our group at Megiddo."

They moved out. Joseph kept a good pace but not working the camels too hard. No stop for midday, they kept on. The sun moved lower as they turned northwest up the valley. The sun set as they neared Megiddo. Joseph saw a fire ahead. "Mary, that must be them!"

They urged the animals on, the beasts straining. Camels panting, Joseph and Mary pulled into the campsite. Alarmed faces looked toward them.

One man shouted. "It is Joseph and Mary!" The campfire emptied, everyone rushing toward the animals. They heeled the camels down and dismounted. One rabbi came forward. "Joseph, you must be exhausted. The men will see to your animals and pitch your tent. Go and eat."

Joseph nodded and the three of them walked to the fire. Yeshua was vibrant and excited, his parents exhausted. They ate like wolves around the fire. Finally Joseph said, "Wife, let us rest. Yeshua, you sleep with us tonight. Come."

They retired to their tent.

The next morning broke crisp and cold. Soon the group stirred, tea and bread shared around a small fire. The head rabbi looked at the men. "We will leave in another hour. Joseph and Mary are not moving. Let us wait. We have plenty of time to make Tiberias." The others nodded.

Yeshua burst out of their tent. Everyone welcomed the boy and gave him food. The women patted the young man on the head. Within an hour his parents emerged. Several of the men approached. "Joseph, get something to eat. Yeshua is with the group. We will pack your tent." Joseph touched his friend on the shoulder.

The group headed northeast through the mountain pass, past the large mounded peak of Mount

Tabor where according to legend Jesus was later "transfigured," appearing with Moses and Elijah. On toward the Sea of Galilee. They arrived in late afternoon and again pitched camp near Tiberias on the water. The rabbis and friends enjoyed each other's company every evening, a bit different than their lives in Nazareth and Sepphoris. They cherished the moments, ever aware it would not last.

The moon shone on the sea and the villages across the water: Magdala, Capernaum, Bethsaida and others sparkled with a few lights.

The next morning the caravan moved up along the shore, then northwest into the hills to home. Magdala lies on the western shore, north of Tiberias. The legendary home of Mary of Magdala (Mary Magdalene). Contrary to popular belief, Mary is never described in the Scriptures as immoral. Jesus cast seven demons out of her, and she figures prominently near the end of his life as one of the women who ministered to him and his group. She and another Mary discovered the empty tomb.

Capernaum is a beautiful setting on the northern shore of the Sea of Galilee. It was always a small village. The "first four" of Jesus' disciples: Peter, Andrew, James and John came from Capernaum or the next-door town of Bethsaida.

The Scriptures state Jesus spent time in Capernaum, as did his mother and brothers. He taught in the local synagogue, recruited followers and although he moved around the Sea, he always returned to Capernaum. The Scriptures say, *"he was in the house."*

Also, *"he was at home."* It seems his family had a dwelling here.

The group arrived in Nazareth, happy to be home. After goodbyes the rest of the caravan traveled the short distance to Sepphoris.

Life settled down. Yeshua continued with synagogue school in Sepphoris, helping Joseph with building and his grandfather with the flocks. But something was wrong. Joseph was slowing down. He began to miss building assignments. Yeshua grew stronger and taller. He took care of both Joseph's work and his own.

After several weeks, one evening as they finished their meal in Sepphoris, Anna and Joseph both excused themselves and retired. Yeshua was left with Joachim. The boy spoke. "Grandfather, something is not right."

The old man looked at his grandson. "What?"

"Father is not well. He is slow, weak. Sometimes he misses work. I have been covering for him."

The old man's eyes fixed on the young man. "How long?"

"Two, maybe three weeks."

"You are sure?"

"I am sure."

Joachim leaned back for a few moments. "Yeshua, say nothing of this to your grandmother or mother. I will check it out. As soon as I know something, I will tell you."

"Yes, Grandfather."

The old man poured the boy some more tea.

Joachim left his flocks to his shepherds and spent more time around Joseph and Yeshua. A week later after evening meal Joseph retired and again the young man and his grandfather were alone. "Yeshua, you were correct as you always seem to be. Joseph is sick. I am not certain but he may be dying. Sometimes people get what we call a 'wasting disease.' This may be one of those. I have spoken to him. Stop doing his work and yours. Take only building jobs for yourself. Do not wear yourself out. It is not fair and our family has plenty of money. You may always help me with the flocks. Most important, stay with your studies."

"All right, Grandfather."

The old man leaned back and drew smoke from his pipe.

Within six months Joseph was dead. He was buried with dignity in Nazareth. Mary and her younger children stood weeping. Joachim, Anna and Yeshua stood apart, solemn and clear-eyed. Mary's oldest son walked to her. "Do not worry, everything will be fine."

"I am not worried, just sad."

"It is the way, Mother. Birth and death. Beginnings and endings. Joseph is gathered to our fathers."

She looked at him. He kissed her on the cheek, put his arm around her shoulders and led her away.

Life went on, as it always does.

Some weeks later Joachim was in the marketplace of Sepphoris, and he encountered the chief rabbi. "Rabbi, how are you?"

"I am fine, how are you?"

"Quite good."

"Tea?"

"Of course."

They found the nearest tea-house and ordered a pot. After a while the rabbi spoke. "Joachim, your grandson."

"Yes, in one or two years he will be finished with schooling."

"He is finished already."

Joachim paused. "What do you mean?"

"We are wasting his time. He is teaching us."

"What are you saying?"

"He must move on."

"Move on to where? He can move into the building trades or help me with the flocks."

"That would be a complete waste of his time. There is greatness is this young man. You know it."

Joachim nodded and looked down. "Of course I know it. Surely you are not thinking of Jerusalem."

"Certainly not ... no, ... Alexandria."

"What? Egypt?"

"Yes. It has the greatest library in the world. I have friends there. He would be in good hands. His fine mind and spirit would expand the way they should."

"His mother will not like this."

"Of course she will not, but she is a good woman, she will come around but it does not matter. That is not your decision or Mary's or mine. The decision is his. It is his life."

"It will be expensive."

The rabbi laughed. "Do not be silly. Give a little less to our synagogue."

Joachim chuckled.

"I know Mary and Joseph have friends in Alexandria from years ago. My friend will provide some income for Yeshua working in the Library."

"Who is your friend?"

"Philo of Alexandria."

"Philo. The heretic!"

"Philo is no heretic. He is a devout Hebrew. A Greek Jew. I grew up with him. He is a fine man. He is simply broad-minded. I would trust him with my life."

Joachim leaned back and was silent, puffing on his pipe. He said, "I will speak with my daughter and Yeshua."

Mary was agitated. "I lost my husband; I have young children and now you want to send my oldest son away!" Her father said nothing. Mary paced around the kitchen, hands slapping her sides. "Who gave you such a crazy idea?"

"The head rabbi."

She stopped walking. "The old man is going soft in his brain! So are you, I think!"

"Why not ask your son what he wants?"

"He is barely fifteen years of age. He is not old enough to make those decisions."

"But he is wise enough. You know it better than anyone else."

"You frustrate the life out of me, Father!"

Joachim looked down. "It was worse for your mother."

"I believe that!" Mary threw her hands in the air and stormed out. Her father went back to his pipe.

The next evening after the meal, Mary spoke. "Father, we want to speak to the rabbi tomorrow."

The old man looked at his grandson. "Yeshua?"

The boy nodded.

The next morning they made their way to the synagogue of Sepphoris. They were ushered to the head rabbi's office; he greeted them and all were seated.

Joachim spoke first. "Rabbi, I have passed your idea to Mary, and she and Yeshua have discussed it." The rabbi looked directly at the boy, went over all the details then said, "Yeshua, we know each other well. You are our prize student. What do you say?"

The boy with his magnetic, unblinking eyes, looked from the rabbi to his grandfather, his grandmother, then Mary, then straight ahead. "I will go."

The rabbi beamed and stood up. Joachim smiled, Anna was placid, Mary's face a blank. The four older people each kissed the young man. Anna's eyes glistened. Mary approached her son, now taller than her. He grasped her shoulders. "Mother, I will return." She grabbed him and burst into tears.

The two women and Yeshua departed. The rabbi looked at his friend. "We should book passage as soon as possible. It is fall; the weather will worsen."

"But we do not know if they will have a place for him."

The rabbi said, "They will make a place. I took the liberty of already sending a message to Philo. Believe me, with what I told him there is no doubt. I will escort the young man to Alexandria. If you wish you may come."

"No, I trust you my friend, and I have no desire to leave Palestine."

"Good. I will book passage for two from Caesarea."

Within ten days they were ready to travel. One of Joachim's servants held the camels steady. It was an emotional farewell. Anna and Mary sobbed. Mary worse. Grandfather's eyes glistened.

The rabbi said, "Yeshua, say your goodbyes. We must depart."

He embraced his family. Joachim and the young one walked to his camel. The old shepherd looked into his grandson's eyes. "We are very proud of you, young man."

"Grandfather, that is the first time you have called me a man."

"It will not be the last." Yeshua mounted the crouched beast and urged him up. The rabbi did the same, then spun and waved to the three silent figures. "Shalom."

"Shalom, Rabbi."

The older man turned and started off. Yeshua swiveled around on the camel and gave a big excited arm-swing to his family. They waved back, then watched until they lost sight of the two travelers.

They moved southwest down the ravine to the Jezreel Valley, then headed south until they came to the main pass leading west to Caesarea Maritima and the sea. Like Sepphoris, Caesarea had developed into a fine city, built by Antipas.

Caesarea

Caesarea on the Mediterranean coast is a magical place. The Crusader ruins of today were built much after the time of Jesus. Well preserved, the castle walls plunge into a now-empty moat for obvious defensive purposes. I was impressed by the "escape hatches," which opened inside the interior walls then dropped down to the outside, emerging under water in the moat. These could be used for people to escape or to appear under water in the moat to secretly infiltrate an attacking force and inflict damage.

*****

The two Galileans, old and young, crested the hill and looked down at the sea. "What do you think, Yeshua?"

The young man's eyes were wide. "It is beautiful." They rested the animals for a time and took in the view. The salt breeze filled their lungs.

"Come, let us find our place." The rabbi spurred his mount with a light rod, and they moved down toward the harbor. The older man knew Caesarea and he headed straight for the synagogue, drawing up outside. Several young men appeared.

"Rabbi Micah, your trip was good?" He urged his camel into a crouch as did Yeshua.

"Yes, I had good company."

The young men looked curiously at this teenage boy they had heard about.

Both dismounted. "Yeshua, are you tired?"

"No, Rabbi, just hungry."

The older man said, "Come, let us find my friends."

They walked to a building north of the synagogue. The rabbi knocked on the door. A man opened it, and his eyes widened. "Micah, you made it here!"

"Do not I always make it?"

"Yeshua, this is Rabbi Hosea. Hosea, this is Yeshua."

57

"So this is the young prodigy," putting his arm around the young man's shoulders. "Come ... Mariah!"

A woman appeared.

"Mariah, please get some food for these two. They are hungry after their journey."

Yeshua was up early the next morning, looking toward the sea as the blue Mediterranean washed ashore in rhythmic waves. The waves flowed up the sand, became thinner and their color changed from dark blue to medium to a light blue until they died on the sand with almost clear water.

Later Micah emerged. "How are you, young man?"

"Wonderful, Rabbi!"

"What would you like to do? We have several days before we sail."

"I want to go to the harbor and see the ships."

"Good, I will see if one of the apprentices can guide you. I will be meeting with my brothers."

Within a short time Micah returned with a young man. "Yeshua, I believe you saw Matthew yesterday. His father was a seaman. He will take you to the port."

Soon the two young men were walking to the boats. Matthew said, "These ships are larger than in Galilee, but the design is similar. Usually one mast and a large sail, sometimes a smaller one on the front end. Normal rudder steering in the rear."

"Do they sail through the seas?"

"They are capable, but if weather is rough they remain near the coast."

The harbor buzzed. People waved and greeted Matthew. He waved back. "Look there Yeshua, that is the kind of craft you and Rabbi will take to Egypt. It is a cargo ship, but it has cabins for passengers."

"Those broader boats are for fishing. They do not travel far."

"What type of fish do they catch?"

"Mullet, grouper, drum, some tuna, sardines."

"Which do you prefer?"

"The smaller fish like sardines. You can eat the whole fish: head, body and tail. It is cheaper, very tasty ... and healthy."

"Come Yeshua, there ... they are bringing in a catch."

The fishermen were emptying nets. Glistening, quivering fish fell out and the men sorted them. The larger, more lucrative ones were separated, the smaller ones shoved aside but not discarded. The young men watched.

"Yeshua, are you hungry?"

"I am becoming hungry."

"Come. I know a clean, cheap fish house nearby."

Soon they sat beside the water and a waiter came to the table.

Matthew said, "What would you like, Yeshua?"

"Whatever you are having."

"Good."

"Waiter, please bring sardines, salad, potatoes, good water."

"Yeshua, do you drink wine?"

"A bit."

"Fine."

"And some white wine, please." The waiter departed.

Matthew said, "I love the action of the waterfront."

"Well, you were born to it."

Matthew chattered on. Finally he stopped. "Yeshua, you do not talk much."

"I learn more listening."

"If you would become a great rabbi, you must talk more. They are all great talkers."

"I never said I wanted to become a rabbi."

Matthew turned. "Then for what reason would you go and study with the greatest rabbi of our world?"

"To learn more of God."

"To what purpose?"

"I just told you the purpose."

Matthew grew silent. After a time Yeshua said, "It is fascinating how they take the boats out to sea. Sometimes they raise the main sail a little and catch a bit of wind. Other times they use the small front sail."

"You have a good eye. The wind is our friend."

Yeshua said, "The wind is the shadow of God. *It blows where it wishes, and we do not know where it comes from or where it is going,* but we sense its strength. So it is with God."

Matthew's eyes narrowed; he looked at Yeshua for some time. At last he said, "We should go."

"Let me share this expense with you."

"No, you are my guest."

The sun declined and a clouded sky rolled in waves over the two young men. They came to the residences. Yeshua said, "Thank you, my friend. I will not forget this day."

"Nor will I. Next time, lunch is on you!"

Yeshua spent the next two evenings with the rabbis, as they talked and shared evening meal. On the last night before departure, Hosea looked at the young man, "Nazarene, you have said little."

Another rabbi interjected, "Tell us, Yeshua. Some say God lives in heaven, some say he lives on earth. Where does he live?"

For a moment the young man stared at the small fire burning in the fireplace. "God lives in heaven and He lives on the earth. He lives in the clouds, in the trees, the flowers and the birds. He lives in the animals and the grass of the fields, and He lives in every person."

The room went silent. Micah looked down and smiled.

Hosea's eyes lifted. After a few moments, he said, "Yeshua, usually one of the rabbis gives our benediction. Would you give it this evening?"

The Nazarene looked and nodded, then he stood and began an ancient verse from the Torah, singing in crystal clear voice, rising then falling, ever confident. The kitchen door opened and several women emerged, eyes and mouths wide and silent, staring at the young chanter. His voice carried on, sailing high then low. Finally he held the last note and it slowly faded away.

After a few moments, Hosea said, "Mariah, please take Yeshua to his quarters. Big day tomorrow." As he walked to the door, he looked back and said, "Shalom, good rabbis and thank you."

Murmurs. "Shalom ... Shalom ... Shalom!"

After some silence one of the rabbis said, "The young man will learn much from Philo."

Micah lifted his head, "And perhaps Philo will learn something ... I have."

Everyone looked at the rabbi as he left.

The next morning, Hosea, Mariah and Matthew accompanied Micah and Yeshua to the port. They found the ship bound for Alexandria, and Matthew made sure their baggage was moved on board. They said their goodbyes.

Matthew said, "Come back, my friend."

"I will."

They boarded the craft and stood at the rail. The boat moved. Yeshua and the rabbi waved goodbye; the ship turned to sea. They went below decks to check their cabin. The baggage was stowed.

"Rabbi, I am going above."

"Be careful."

"Of course."

He bounced out of the room.

The rabbi headed up to the deck. The ship swayed in the waves tilting left and driving southwest, the wind billowing the sails. Near the front of the boat Yeshua hung to the rigging, face in the wind, hair blowing like the dark flag atop the main mast. Micah grabbed the railing and moved forward. "How is it, young one?" he yelled.

Yeshua looked back, grinning from ear to ear. "Magnificent!" He pointed his face forward again. Micah gripped the railing, rubbed the young man's curly hair and thought, *"If I had a son, I would want one like this."* They stood for a time, wind screaming past as the sun reached its peak.

The rabbi said, "Yeshua, I am going below to steady my legs and get a bit of food to settle my stomach."

"I will be along in a while."

"Do not let the sun burn you."

"No sir."

It was three nights on the ship before they neared the Nile Delta, the morning of the fourth day. The great Pharos of Alexandria loomed ahead. "Look, Rabbi, the lighthouse. I remember from when I was young."

"You remember back a long time."

The Pharos rose like a giant chess piece, five levels, each narrowing until the final tower surged toward the heavens. During the day great mirrors reflected the sun's brilliance from the top. At sundown fires inside the top cast light on the mirrors reflecting in every direction as plumes of smoke sprouted from the top openings, like fluffy white flower petals.

The boat angled left into the harbor, the sail coming down. They anchored, mooring ropes shooting out like rifle shots. Deckhands grabbed and secured them. The two Galileans disembarked, took their bags and moved to the land end of the pier, legs adjusting to steadiness underfoot. "Rabbi, let me take your bag; it is heavier." Micah smiled as they traded.

After a short walk the rabbi halted. "Well there it is Yeshua, right before us. The Great Library."

"I remember."

To the left a castle-like structure with two turrets thrust upward. In the center of the city complex, two massive towers erupted both wide and high. Between the towers near the front of the sprawling expanse was another tall tower, much slimmer. The lower walls of the Library spread right.

"Rabbi, these parts of the city look so different in style."

"Because they were built at different times as things grew. There were fires, certain sections replaced when needed and there were different influences over the years. Greek, Hebrew, Egyptian."

They walked left toward the Jewish quarter. Micah said, "Wait, I will ask directions."

"I believe I remember, Rabbi."

"You were very young. You remember?"

"I think so." They walked a bit. "Here is the street."

Micah looked at his piece of parchment. Yeshua walked ahead. At the fifth door on the right he stopped and knocked. It opened.

Miriam was older, her face more full and lined. For a moment she simply stared, then her eyes filled. "Yeshua! You did come back!" She grabbed and squeezed him so tightly he almost choked. Then she spun him around several times. "We could not believe you were really coming!"

The older man stepped forward. "I am Rabbi Micah."

"Yes, of course. Welcome. Shalom." She bowed slightly and grasped his hand. Then she turned. "Yari, they are here!" He appeared. His hair was now white, his beard salt and pepper, the same twinkle in his eyes. "Yeshua, you are brown as a nut. After all these years, you have returned." A big hug. "Look at you! Almost a man!"

Miriam said, "Yari, this is Rabbi Micah."

"Rabbi, you are welcome as long as you wish to stay!"

"Thank you, I believe a week or so would be more than enough to get Yeshua settled with my friends at the Library."

"Of course." Yari clapped his hands and a servant appeared. "Show these two men to their rooms and carry the rabbi's bags." The three of them disappeared.

Miriam and Yari rested in the atrium. Soon Yeshua reappeared, and the couple rose. The young man grinned from ear to ear. "Aunt, Uncle, I am so happy to be back!"

"Not as happy as we are," said Yari. "You must stay with us, unless of course you are determined to stay at the Library."

"That is most kind and gracious. I much prefer to stay with you. I want a little balance in my life."

They laughed. Miriam said, "Wonderful, it is settled then. Yeshua, are you hungry?"

"Yes."

"Good. You men get reacquainted. I will prepare something. What about the rabbi?"

"He is resting."

She headed for the kitchen. Yari motioned to sit.

"Yeshua, tell me about your life since you abandoned us." The young man chuckled and began. Yari listened while he spoke of his youth, the synagogue teaching, helping his grandfather with the flocks, learning to build with Joseph, tiny Nazareth, blossoming Sepphoris, his brothers and sisters, Jerusalem, the Sea of Galilee, his journey back to Egypt, on and on. He stopped.

Yari was silent for a time. "You know, Yeshua, most people in cities like Alexandria believe 'country people' like you are quiet, naive, maybe uninteresting. You will surprise this city."

Miriam entered with a platter of food: meats, bread, tomatoes, cheese, olive oil, dates, a saucer of salt, a pot of tea. She placed it on the table and the other two moved to join her. Yari said, "Blessed, O Lord our God who gives us bread to eat." They began to partake.

The next morning both Yeshua and the rabbi were up early to depart for the Library. After a short breakfast they set out, traveling west along the water from the Hebrew sector toward the Library. The harbor was a blur of ships, dock-hands, businesses looking at the sea. The sun rose in their faces.

They neared the Pharos peninsula, and the Library stretched on their left. At the main entrance Micah looked at the attendant and said, "We have an appointment with Rabbi Philo."

"Your names, please."

"Rabbi Micah and Yeshua."

"One moment please." He departed.

The attendant came back. "Rabbi Philo will see you now. This way please." He led them through a vast hall, parchments in cases towering above them. Passing through a large area they veered left and came to a series of offices. The attendant rapped on a door.

"Come."

He pushed on the entrance and beckoned for the two to enter. A serious looking man with a headpiece sat behind a large desk. He looked up, rose and beamed. "Micah, Shalom! He circled the desk and grabbed the other man. Air kisses on both cheeks. "How was the voyage?"

"All right, I am not the best sailor. Yeshua here was fine."

Philo looked at the young man. "So you are the one Micah has spoken so highly of. Welcome!"

"Thank you, Rabbi."

"Well young man, we will put you to work with the clerks, copying manuscripts in Greek and Hebrew. How does that sound?"

"Fine, sir."

"Very well. You are dismissed. I must talk to my old friend. Please wait outside."

He departed and the two men talked for some time.

Yeshua settled into the routine. Every day he arrived in the morning and copied manuscripts until mid-afternoon. After work he found his way to the city gymnasium where he began to exercise and wrestle with the athletes, both Greek and Hebrew. Some months passed. Philo regularly met with his clerks. After a time he asked the head clerk, "How is the young Galilean doing?"

"Excellent, Rabbi. His copies are flawless in both Hebrew and Greek, and his writing is beautiful and straight as an arrow."

The next day Philo summoned Yeshua to his office.

"Yes, Rabbi?"

"Yeshua, I am moving you to the translators. Isaias here is head of the section. He will be your supervisor. Is that all right?"

"Yes sir."

"Good. You are dismissed."

After six months, Philo was having a meeting with his translators. As the meeting concluded he said, "Isaias, remain please."

"How is the Galilean doing? The truth."

"He is the best I have. Greek to Hebrew. Hebrew to Greek. I already give him the most important work."

"Thank you. Send him to me."

Within a few minutes Yeshua appeared. "Yes, Rabbi?"

"Please sit. Would you like some tea?"

"I am fine, sir."

"I want you to be my personal assistant."

"What does that involve, Rabbi?"

"You would help me with my work. The writing, the grammar, making any suggestions you deem appropriate, other matters necessary in the office."

"I am very honored, sir."

"Then you accept."

"Gladly."

"Yeshua, I am the one who is honored. You have accepted every task for the past year, no matter how humble and performed flawlessly. Everyone enjoys working with you. Micah was correct about you. How are Yari and Miriam?"

"They are fine."

"They must be happy having you with them."

"They are."

Philo smiled, "Be here tomorrow morning. You are dismissed."

Yeshua walked by the sea as he often did in evening. The sun and clouds cast a deep red glow as he arrived home. He saw Miriam in the atrium. "How was your day, dear one?," she asked.

"Fine, Aunt. I will tell you at dinner."

Later as the three of them ate, Yeshua told them what happened today. Miriam leaped to her feet and embraced the young man. "Oh, Yeshua, this is such an honor. You will be Philo's assistant!"

Yari sat quietly. He said, "Yeshua, Miriam and I are at the center of the Hebrew community here. Since you arrived, we have been more discreet with our parties and festivities. We did not want to overwhelm you. No more. This next Thursday before Sabbath we will have a celebration here. The purpose will be unstated but it will be obvious. Please invite any of your friends you wish. We are very proud of you!"

The next Thursday at sundown guests arrived. Soon the house overflowed. As did the tables of food. A lyre began pouring out a deep, rhythmic melody that made everyone want to dance. A circle formed in the atrium and arm-in-arm it began to spin with dignity and grace. Time dissolved. It could have been centuries in the past or centuries in the future. It was *now*.

Yeshua sat with Yari, Miriam and some of his gymnasium friends, then someone grabbed and dragged him into the dance group. Soon he was in the circle, clutching the arms of partners right and left, legs moving in harmony, pausing, kicking. Mediterranean dancing tends to be extended, but at last the lyre died and the group disbanded.

Yeshua returned and sat beside Miriam. She said, "So you know how to dance."

"Even in the country they teach us some things."

Their home had a large garden in the rear and after everyone had enough food, guests began to circulate throughout the house and the garden. Yari and Philo approached. "Yeshua, I am honored to have you as assistant."

"The honor is mine, sir." The older men walked away.

The young man strolled to the garden, smelling the flowers, enjoying the sky. He turned and a young woman was before him.

"Hello Yeshua."

"Hello."

"I am Esther."

"I know who you are."

"How do you know?"

"I have seen you at synagogue."

"Oh, I did not know you had noticed."

"You are a good dancer."

Esther asked, "How could you tell? We were in a group."

"I can see who is well coordinated."

"I have heard this about you. You are well coordinated."

"Where have you heard such a thing?"

"I have heard of your prowess at the gymnasium."

"Oh."

"Congratulations on your promotion. It is a great honor."

"Would you like to walk?"

"Certainly."

They moved among the plants and flowers and trees, chatting easily, laughing a bit. They came face to face with Miriam and Yari. "So Yeshua, I see you find the good people."

Esther's cheeks reddened a bit and Yari took her arm. "Come my dear, let us see if there is any food or dancing left." Miriam hooked her nephew's arm. They made their way to the atrium. The party was breaking up. People said goodbyes. Esther's parents approached. "Miriam, Yari, thank you for a lovely evening. Young

Yeshua, much congratulations on your recent promotion."

"Thank you."

Esther's large eyes looked at the young man. "Good night, Yeshua."

"Good night, Esther."

They were gone.

He settled into his job as Philo's assistant. Soon he helped with the writing. Even making suggestions about phrasing. The older man was not stubborn. He welcomed the aid.

One day after a month the rabbi and Yeshua worked on a difficult translation. Philo threw down his quill. "Young man, I am exhausted. Are you hungry?"

"Yes."

"Let us go." It was the first time the scholar suggested eating together. They walked from the office. The rabbi moved toward the entrance.

Yeshua said, "Not the cafeteria?"

"Enough work for today. I know a good place." Outside they walked toward the Hebrew quarter. Philo pointed, "There, those tables by the water."

The manager greeted them. "Shalom, Rabbi. It is good to see you." Philo said, "You also. How about that table on the water?"

"Of course." He walked ahead, feet crunching across the gravel, quickly prepared the table and they sat.

A waiter appeared. "Hello, sir. What may I get you?"

"May we see your fish?"

"Of course." He headed toward the display table. A good variety of fish and crustaceans were arranged in the shade. They still glistened.

Philo looked over the table and his eyes stopped. "You have barbouni?"

"Yes. Fresh this morning."

The older man said, "Yeshua, have you had barbouni?"

"No."

"You have to try this. It is a type of goatfish or mullet, as you can see, pink in color, slightly sweet. I acquired a taste for this when I studied in Athens."

"Fine."

"What else would you like?"

"Whatever you are having."

"White wine?"

"A little."

"Good!" They went back to their table. Soon the food arrived: rice, vegetables, bread, wine and the grilled barbouni. Philo said a short blessing and they both dug in with enthusiasm.

Yeshua said, "The fish is wonderful!"

"You see young man, I know something other than scrolls and parchments."

They finished the meal and the sun declined. "Let us go, Yeshua." They walked west along the water toward the Library. "Rabbi, this is my street. Would you like me to walk further with you?"

"No, I am not decrepit. Not yet. Shalom, my young assistant."

"Shalom."

Several weeks later Yeshua returned with three Greek friends after a workout in the gymnasium. A young woman walked toward them. His eyes widened and he picked up his pace, separating from his companions.

"Esther?"

She looked up, "Yeshua, how are you?"

"Fine. I miss the parties ... and dancing."

"As do I."

"Perhaps you could ask your parents to have a festivity."

"They are not good at socializing. Not like your uncle and aunt."

"Then I will speak to them tonight."

"Good."

His friends caught up. They could not take their eyes off Esther. "Hebrew, will you not introduce us to your friend?"

Yeshua looked at them evenly. "This is a proper young woman. I would never introduce her to the three of you!"

"Bah!" They laughed and jeered, waving their hands.

He looked back. "It is good to see you, Esther."

"The same."

"What is in the bag?"

"Vegetables for the meal tonight. My mother is a good cook."

"As I am sure her daughter is. Do you need some help?"

"I am fine. Shalom, Yeshua."

"Shalom."

She turned and walked away. He watched her then caught up with his friends."

One of the Greeks said, "So, our Jewish friend is not such the Stoic he pretends. Who was that charming creature?"

"None of your business."

Another of the Greeks said, "Do you wrestle with her also?"

Yeshua gave him a wry look, "I told you she is respectable."

"Yes, but we always hope you are not!"

One friend shoved him sideways. Another grabbed him around the shoulders. The last one tussled his hair. They kept moving, laughing, joking. Esther stopped and looked for a moment, smiled, then resumed her walk.

Within several weeks there was another party at the home of Yari and Miriam. The young and older people danced in a circle in the atrium. Esther was often at Yeshua's side. Other young girls tried to grasp his other arm. Often Middle Eastern dancing seems like a marathon. At last there was a pause and Yeshua leaned forward and grasped his knees.

"Esther, are you thirsty?"

"Yes!" She looked at him, face shining.

"Let us get some lemon drink." He walked to the table, picked up two cups of juice and handed one to her. She walked toward her parents and sat. Yeshua followed her. Yari and Miriam sat close by.

Esther's father said, "Young man, you will not need the gymnasium tomorrow. You have had quite enough exercise tonight." Yeshua nodded and took another sip. After a time he said, "Esther, I am still warm. Perhaps the garden will be cooler." Esther stood. "Father, please excuse us." He nodded.

As they moved away, Esther's father asked, "Yari, what kind of man is he?"

"The best I have seen."

"Are you sure my daughter is safe with him?"

"I am not sure of anything. But I know no young man I would trust more."

Yari leaned over and touched goblets with his friend. "We can ask no more."

Esther's father replied, "Nor should we."

The two young people walked through the hallway to the garden. It was not much cooler. "Esther, let us find where the breeze is best."

"All right."

"Look. There is a marble bench." They sat and were silent for a time.

Esther said, "Something is bothering you, Yeshua."

"I miss my home."

"Your family?"

"And the country. I feel at peace there. Close to God."

"I see."

After a few moments Esther said, "We should get back."

"Sure."

They went to the atrium, Esther walking slightly ahead. The crowd thinned. Esther's mother said, "We should say our goodbyes." The young woman bade farewell to Yari, kissed Miriam on the cheek and whispered something in her ear.

Several nights later after evening meal Miriam said, "You are homesick, Yeshua."

"You have been speaking with Esther."

"As usual, you are very perceptive," said Yari. "You have been here over a year. You should go home for a month. We certainly can afford the voyage, and I am sure Philo will give you the time off."

Yeshua's eyes shone. He rose, walked to Miriam and kissed her on the forehead. "If you will excuse me, I will retire."

Within a week they were at the harbor. Yari grabbed Yeshua's bag and walked to one of the stewards. "Is this the ship for Caesarea Maritima?"

"Yes, sir."

Yari slipped him a few coins. "Please stow this bag in my nephew's cabin. Yeshua of Nazareth."

"Yes, sir."

Yari returned to his wife and the young man. Esther and her parents approached from the city. Her mother kissed Yeshua on the cheek. "Goodbye, young man."

"Goodbye, Madam."

Esther's father extended his hand. "Be safe, Yeshua."

"Yes, sir."

Miriam stepped forward and put arms around her nephew. "Come back to us." He looked at her without expression and nodded.

Yari grabbed the young man. "Take care ... and watch out for those Galilean rascals."

"I know how to handle them."

Esther stepped forward and gave him a respectable hug. "I will miss seeing you, Yeshua of Nazareth."

He smiled at her. "It will only be one month." He turned, walked up the gangplank then moved forward on the ship, stopped and gazed at the five of them.

Esther's mother asked, "Miriam, will he be back?"

Esther interrupted, "He will return."

Miriam looked sideways, "How can you be so sure?"

"He just told me."

The four older people stared at Esther without speaking. She looked at the Nazarene, gripping the rail, staring at them. The ship began to move. The young woman raised her hand. Yeshua grinned and raised his. They began to wave. He simply stood at the rail. The ship turned toward the sea and they lost sight of him. The large sail billowed; the craft gained speed. Soon it was a brown and white speck on a deep blue rolling carpet, white cotton clouds moving above with the wind. The boat swerved, moving the same direction as the clouds.

He spent the next few days topside as much as he could, chatting with deck hands, asking about their work. Growing up in Nazareth, working with shepherds and craftsmen, studying with noted rabbis, highly intelligent but no airs about him. He showed interest in whatever a person did or said. Most were glad someone gave them any attention.

Several days later they landed at Caesarea. The ship pulled to the dock. Hosea, Mariah and Matthew were on the pier. Yeshua waved from the boat. As soon as the craft secured, he was the first one off.

Matthew said, "Here Galilean, give me your bag." Mariah and Hosea went to each side of the young man, and they each put their arm around his now broad shoulders. Mariah asked, "Tell me, can you still chant?"

"A little bit."

The rabbi chuckled, "I doubt it is a little!" They walked toward the synagogue. At evening they sat in Mariah's kitchen. Eating, talking. Hosea said, "Yeshua, your grandfather sent a camel driver and an extra animal. You may leave for Nazareth as soon as you are ready."

Matthew stood and put up his hands. "Wait! He owes me a lunch!" Laughter.

Yeshua looked at his friend. "You are a good Hebrew, Matthew. You keep close accounts!"

Two days later they sat at the same seaside eatery. As they ate, Matthew asked, "How is it in Alexandria?"

"Good. Very busy. Plenty of work. It is a Greek and Hebrew city."

"There is no problem with the Greeks?"

"Not much. I have Greek friends."

"You have Greek friends?!"

"Yes, some in the Library, some in the gymnasium."

"You socialize with them?"

"Only what I said. I socialize with our people and of course I keep the Sabbath. How are things here?"

"Things never change here. The Romans and the Temple priests control everything, and they have their foot on our neck. I have a favor to ask. If I left Palestine, came to Alexandria, could you find me a place?"

"A place?"

"A job, a livelihood."

Yeshua looked at him for a moment. "Of course, ... without a doubt. I have friends in the Library, friends in the synagogue, my uncle is a prominent businessman. No problem. We would get you started."

Matthew hung his head and patted his friend's arm.

Two mornings later he was ready to depart. The camel driver waited with an extra mount. Yeshua looked at his three friends. "Thank you for your hospitality."

He mounted his camel and urged it up. They headed away. After a few meters, the young man waved. Hands signaled back. They took the most direct route. North along the coast, through the pass to Jezreel. The camel driver turned north. Yeshua said, "Wait!"

"What is it?"

"The most direct route to Nazareth is this way."

"Your grandfather said come to Sepphoris."

"My mother, brothers and sisters are waiting in Nazareth. Do not worry. My grandfather will understand. No blame will come to you. We go to Nazareth."

"All right." He spurred east. The sun set as they pulled in. Yeshua prodded his camel into a crouch and it bellowed. Mary and a bunch of children half the size of Yeshua, flew out of the house.

"Son! Is it you?!"

"Yes, Mother." They hugged a long time. Then he kneeled and embraced the children, rubbing their hair. He looked at the driver. "Go immediately to Sepphoris. Tell my grandfather I will see him tomorrow. Leave my animal." He rode off. Yeshua looked at the tallest boy. "Can you hobble a camel?" He nodded. "Please do, I am tired." Mary led her oldest son inside. The candles burned a long time.

Although he slept soundly, Yeshua was up by mid-morning, looking over the valley to Sepphoris, watching his grandfather's flocks. Mary brought him a cup of tea and they sat together. "I have missed you, Mother." She put her arm on his shoulder. "I know."

"The children are beautiful."

She squeezed his shoulder. "So are you. Are you hungry?"

"Yes."

"Come, I will make you some eggs." She rose and went inside. After eating he said, "Mother, I will go see Grandfather. How is he?"

"Fine. He never changes." Yeshua kissed her on the cheek and left. The oldest of his younger brothers was near the camel. "You must be James."

"Yes."

"Thank you for hobbling the camel last night. I am going to see Grandfather. Would you like to come?"

"Oh, yes!"

"Go, ask Mother."

Soon he returned. "James, get behind me, on the animal. Hold on." They rose. Mary watched from the doorway as the two brothers headed down the hill toward Sepphoris. Soon they were among the flocks and drew up to the first shepherd. "Where is Joachim?"

"Who are you?"

Yeshua swung the camel and the boy behind him said, "This is my brother!"

"Well hello, young man. Your grandfather is there on the next ridge." He urged the beast on, then drew up to the men on the rise and prodded his mount down. Joachim looked up and smiled.

"Shalom, Grandfather." There were tears in the old man's eyes. "And who is this young camel driver with you?"

"Oh, I found him wandering around the village up there."

"Come, your grandmother is anxious to see you."

Yeshua turned. "Young camel driver, ride that beast to your grandfather's house."

"Me?"

"I do not see any other camel drivers here." Yeshua put his arm around Joachim's shoulders and they walked toward the house.

"How are things in Alexandria, Son?"

"They are fine, Grandfather. Philo is the greatest Hebrew scholar; he treats me well. Yari and Miriam are great family. The city is fascinating and peaceful. I have made good friends."

"But you miss your home. You miss Palestine."

"Yes."

Joachim patted his shoulder. "You will figure it out."

Anna was in her garden and she saw them walking. "Yeshua!" He ran to her and they embraced for a long time.

For the next several weeks Yeshua split his time between his grandparents and his family in Nazareth. He enjoyed getting to know his seven brothers and sisters, playing and joking with them and spending time with his grandfather and the flocks. It was good to be in the countryside after so much city time.

One pleasant evening the extended family, almost a dozen souls gathered at the Nazareth house in late afternoon. Two spits, one with a lamb and one with a goat spun over fires. The smell of roasting meat drifted through the breeze, tables and chairs spread around the cooking area. Yeshua sat with one of his young sisters and looked out over the valley toward Sepphoris, lights sparkling as the sun set behind it.

"Rachel, I hear you are a good student at the synagogue school."

"Yes, I like school. Perhaps one day I will go to Alexandria like you."

"The synagogue in Sepphoris is growing, and they have good rabbis and teachers here."

"Then why did you leave?"

"I believed I could learn more there."

"Have you?"

"In some ways. I study with a great Rabbi in both Hebrew and Greek. After a while it does not matter. Knowledge becomes the same in any language. Wisdom is another thing."

"What is the difference?"

"Knowledge is in the mind. Wisdom involves the heart. I have met people whose minds are full of knowledge but they are foolish." Music began to play in the background. "Come young lady, perhaps you can teach me a Palestinian dance I have forgotten." They stood and moved toward the music. He waited until Rachel reached up for his hand and he let her begin. They danced for a few minutes, then the smaller sister, Leah, grabbed his other hand. He laughed, "I have two lovely dancing partners!"

After a short time he said, "You have worn me out. Go teach someone else to dance." He walked to the tables, took some grilled meat and wine and found a seat looking at the valley. Two other brothers, Simon and Judah, joined him. Judah said, "It is a beautiful evening." Yeshua nodded. Simon spoke, "Brother, will you let us ride the camel, like you did James?"

"If Mother says it is all right."

"Mother protects us too much."

Yeshua looked at them. "We have the best mother in the world."

The next morning he sat in the same spot sipping tea, his camel hobbled nearby. Simon and Judah joined him. "Are you two ready to ride a camel?" They almost jumped up together. The three of them walked to the animal and Yeshua un-hobbled him. "Come on, you two get behind me. You do not look like you weigh too much." They started down the slope toward Sepphoris, the oldest brother talking about how to handle a camel. They came near where Joachim spoke with some stewards. Yeshua moved the camel into crouch and they dismounted. "All right Simon, grab the reins. Take him up the rise then return, not too fast." Simon moved out, big grin on his face. "Judah, let us watch. He is holding his ropes all right, a little tight. See how the camel's head is arching back a bit. Now watch as he spins him around ... not bad."

Simon returned. Yeshua helped him get the animal down. "All right Judah, your time." Judah followed the same path giving the camel just a bit more rein. His turn a little wider. He stopped before his brothers. "Go ahead, see if you can bring him into to a crouch." The animal came down.

The boys were excited. "Let us go again!"

"No, enough. If something happens, I will be to blame."

Three weeks went by. One night as the two youngest boys played a game with their oldest brother, Mary appeared. "Time for bed."

"Oh, Mother, we were beating him!"

"To bed."

Mary looked at her son, "You are leaving."

"It is time."

Within a week Yeshua was on a boat sailing to Egypt. It pulled into harbor and Esther waited on the dock. Yeshua disembarked and embraced her. She said, "Where are your uncle and aunt?"

"They do not know I am arriving today."

"I am the only one you told?"

He picked up his bag and they walked toward the city, falling into their normal chatter. She slid her arm through his. They neared the Hebrew quarter. He said, "This is your street."

"I know where I live, Yeshua of Nazareth."

"Thank you for coming to the boat."

"Thank you for the escort home." She walked several doors to her home, glancing sideways at him before she entered.

Yeshua went back to his routine, which he very much enjoyed. Every year he went to Palestine for a month. After several years one day Philo said, "I have been invited to speak at the Library of Antioch."

The young man's eyes widened. "It is a great honor!"

"What do you know about that Library?"

"I heard it spawned ours. Manuscripts brought from Antioch to start the Library here."

"One story. Perhaps. It is more sure that manuscripts were acquired from the Library at Pergamon and the book markets of Athens and Rhodes. In any event I was invited and I want you to come with me."

"Come with you! Why?"

"You know how much I rely on you. Also it is on the way past Palestine. Perhaps you can include your annual visit."

"Sounds great!"

Within a month they were on their way. A short stop in Cyprus then on to Antioch, Greater Syria.

*****

I have been to Adana in modern day Turkey, about one hundred miles from Antioch. Some people say East meets West in Athens. Depends how you measure such things but to me, Athens is more western. Some say East meets West in Istanbul. I would say the international airport in Istanbul is more western, the domestic airport more eastern and the rest of the city a similar mix. But when I visited Adana Turkey, I knew the balance had shifted East.

We landed on a business trip with a flight from Italy, and I was anxious to enjoy Greek-style food. Greek and Turkish food are quite similar for some obvious historical reasons. There is a wonderful Greek dip known as *tzatziki*, a cucumber/yoghurt/garlic spread I grew to adore from my years living in Greece. I remember one evening in Athens after I and two friends had been to a Greek *taverna* enjoying the garlic dip, we showed up at the home of some older American friends. The lady of the house opened the door and after about ten seconds she said, "I perceive you boys have just come from a restaurant. Keep your distance." Funny, we didn't notice it.

Our host in Adana asked if we wanted to stop at a local restaurant after our flight landed and we heartily agreed. It was early evening and I overdid it on the *tzatziki*. I'm sure it was the change to Turkish dairy (the yoghurt). Next day I was sick as a dog. I wasn't much good for the rest of the business trip.

The next day we took an excursion to a nearby village nestled at the bottom of a hill, upon which perched the ruins of a Crusaders' fort. My buddies were keen on climbing to the ruins. I deferred, deciding to just hang out at the base. Soon about six very cute Turkish children surrounded me. They seemed to enjoy being around, laughing and chattering although we shared nothing in common in language. I noticed a man and a woman not far away. He was dressed in what could have been a western style: nice trousers, dress shirt, sweater. The woman seemed almost in Gypsy-like garb, loose, colorful wrappings, some sort of headpiece.

My friends returned from their hike and my boss, an Air Force flight surgeon who spoke Turkish said, "Well, you made some friends." I nodded, which after the previous night was about all I wanted to do.

I did say, "It was nice these kids and their friends hung out with me."

He said, "They are all brothers and sisters. Those are the parents."

I realized if I had lined them up, each child would be about three inches shorter than the preceding one. I asked my boss, "How many people in this village?"

"Maybe a thousand or so."

"How many houses?"

"I don't know. A hundred?"

"I see."

Antioch

Antioch was an important town for followers of the "Way" after the crucifixion of Jesus. Paul made several visits, including one with Barnabas and once when he met Peter here. They disagreed about something religious people of the same faith always seem to find to argue about.

The Library of Antioch was prominent at this time, as were the Libraries of Pergamon and Alexandria. The Library of Athens had gone away but it would later revive. Great Libraries often had a museum attached, which makes sense to us today. They also often had a gymnasium, which seems odd until we realize that back in those centuries, development of the body ranked in the same realm as development of the mind. The emphasis today on wholistic health is nothing new. We simply must travel back in time.

Today the city of Antioch (now Antakya) lies in present day Turkey, not Greater Syria as it did in the past. Although the city is only a bit over 200,000 in population, Mustafa Kemal University has around 30,000 students. Learning lives on here.

To this day Antioch has a reputation for miracles and magic, spirits and spells. So it was in the time of Jesus. You can read it through the New Testament. This is often how wonder-workers validated themselves back then, and they were generally well paid for their services. Time travel. Jesus was unusual with his miracles. He did not charge for them.

*****

Philo and Yeshua made their way to the Great Library and they were well received. Over the next few days the rabbi gave his lectures. After he finished he asked, "Yeshua, did you find this boring? We work on this all the time."

"No, it was good to see how you synthesize and condense all this, the Greek and the Hebrew, and how you speak with allegory, the same way you write." Philo glanced at the younger man.

Soon they were on another ship heading south to Caesarea Maritima. When they docked, Matthew and Hosea were waiting on the pier. "Philo, it is wonderful to finally meet you. I was thrilled when I received the message you were coming."

"Thank you, perhaps I will see what is so fascinating here to my assistant." They moved toward the synagogue. Hosea spoke, "Yeshua, as usual your grandfather has sent a camel driver and an extra mount."

Philo decided to stay a week. There was talk of starting a new Library in Caesarea, and Hosea was delighted to have Philo's inputs. Yeshua stayed two days, and he and Matthew spent time together. Sitting by the water, Yeshua said, "Matthew, usually you are the talkative one. What is it?"

"Oh, it never changes here."

"Do not expect it to. I have told you, you have a place in Egypt."

"I love it here."

"As do I. That is the dilemma."

Soon Yeshua was on his way to Nazareth. He again settled in with his family. His brothers and sisters adored him. His mother was thrilled. His grandparents seemed ageless.

This time he did not stray far from Nazareth, but something agitated him. When his month was almost up, one evening as he and Mary gazed toward Sepphoris she asked, "What is it, Son?"

"Mother, you know how much I love you and our family. How much I love this land. But I know how pressured you are, how heavily you are taxed."

"All my life Son, long before you were born, it has been this way."

"That is not the best."

"Good, better, best. Do you really think we can expect the best?"

"No, but we can hope for better."

"Hope yes, but hope is a tenuous thing."

Within a week Yeshua was on a ship bound for Alexandria. He settled back into his routine. One day he sat in the gymnasium with his Greek friends when a very dark young man entered. Dimitri said, "Who in Hades is he?"

Yanni said, "Looks like an Arab. No one will wrestle with him."

The Nazarene stood. "Well, not no one."

"Yeshua, you have already had two matches."

He moved toward the dark boy. "What is your name?"

"Ismael. You?"

"Yeshua."

"You are Hebrew?"

"Yes, for a long time. Do you wrestle?"

"Yes."

"You look my size. Let us give it a go. Over there."

Yeshua moved to the mat and signaled to the referee. He nodded.

The two young men squared off. The Arab lunged and Yeshua deftly kicked him aside. He rolled to the edge of the mat.

"Do not charge, you make it too easy."

The Egyptian's face was red and his eyes angry. He squared off again, then tried to catch hold of an arm. Yeshua grabbed his head, pushed him down and stepped aside.

"Do not lead with your eyes. Anyone can see it."

The Arab's face went blank. He moved left, faked right, then went for the waist. He managed to hold on. Yeshua strained back, but the dark man had a decent grip. They tumbled down. The Hebrew flipped on top and quickly pinned the Egyptian. The referee slapped the mat. It was over.

Yeshua reached down with his arm and lifted the Arab. "You were easy on me."

"Yes, not tomorrow."

"Some day, I will wrestle the best here."

Yeshua looked at him. "You just did." He walked away.

The Greeks were laughing. One said, "Yeshua, why are you so kind?"

He put his arm on his friend's shoulder. "Dimitri, if you are not kind, what good are you?"

Another two years passed. One day, Philo said, "Yeshua, I am going to Greece to acquire more manuscripts. Would you like to come?"

"Of course. Where?"

"Definitely Rhodes and Athens. Perhaps Pergamon, but I doubt they will have much they want to give up."

Within two weeks they were on a ship bound for Rhodes.

Rhodes

Rhodes, like Alexandria during this time was part of the Roman Empire. The island is shaped like a dolphin, swimming toward the coast of Asia Minor. The capital city of Rhodes Town is perched on the snout. Long known as an intellectual center, a place of refuge and exile for elite Romans, high society. Known for rhetoric and so, a location of private library manuscripts.

Philo and Yeshua landed in the great harbor which once held the massive "Colossus of Rhodes," the giant bronze statue that many images show straddling the harbor entrance. This is idealistic, most likely inaccurate. It probably stood beside the port until an earthquake took it down in 224 BC. Like the Great Library of Alexandria it was one of the Seven Wonders of the Ancient World. There was a prominent Jewish community here and the two Alexandrians felt at home. They roamed about the booksellers, and Philo made some wise purchases for the Library.

After he had done as much buying as seemed prudent, they relaxed one evening at a *taverna* near the harbor. "Yeshua, there is a play tomorrow evening at the great theater in Lindos. We should go."

"Which play?"

"I do not know. Some Greek drama like we have in Alexandria. They say the site is magnificent. Southeast side of the island. We would have to stay overnight. There is also a classic Greek temple dedicated to Athena and wonderful views over the bay."

"Fine."

"Good. I will make the arrangements."

By afternoon the next day they were at Lindos. The temple site was stunning, atop a promontory looking down at a picturesque bay. On the far downward slope was the huge amphitheater. Yeshua said, "I am going down for a swim."

"I will go with you."

"To swim?"

"Bah! I will have some wine and watch you."

They hired two donkeys and headed down the slope. Soon Yeshua was in the sea, swimming far out in calm waters, then turning and coming back. Some Greek female swimmers watched him. He grabbed a cloth, wiped his face and sat down at a seaside table with Philo.

"You attract an audience."

"I had not noticed."

Philo said, "Do not play with me, young man. I know you too well."

"You know there is only one woman for me."

"Yes, I know. I am going to order some fish. Are you hungry?"

"Yes, but I will take another swim."

"A long one?"

"No, a short dip."

"Good, I will order the fish."

Yeshua moved toward the bay. Philo motioned to the waiter.

In fifteen minutes as the waiter brought the food Yeshua emerged from the water. He toweled himself off. "What is the fish? Even smaller than sardines."

"Marides." Philo divided the food onto two plates. They dug in.

Early evening they entered the amphitheater. Philo motioned to some seats near the top.

"You do not want to sit closer?"

"No, it is much cooler up high. Besides the acoustics in Greek theaters are so great, if someone snapped their fingers down on the stage, you would hear it up here."

The performance was superb. Afterwards they retired to their inn.

*****

I have been to Rhodes numerous times during several seasons of the year. In Greece it is known as "Sunshine Island" with 300 days of sun a year (bring your skin protector). The most striking aspect of the island is the ancient center of Rhodes Town, sitting at the northern end of the island. One of the finest medieval relics in the world, built long after the time of Jesus.

It was constructed by the Knights of St. John Hospitallers, a Roman Catholic religious order, which established hospitals in Italy and on the way to Jerusalem. Like the Templars, the Knights were active during the Crusades. They morphed into a military order. The knights were divided into seven different "tongues" based on the various European languages each group spoke. When they were forced out of Jerusalem, the Knights moved to Cyprus then took up residence on

Rhodes for about 200 years in the Middle Ages. They constructed the marvelous old city, which is extremely well preserved, a UNESCO World Heritage Center. To walk the Street of the Knights, their Palace and the hospital, now an archeological museum, is to stroll back in time.

A drained moat circles the old city and I was delighted to see some of the small fallow deer, unique to Rhodes, roaming around the trench. Legend says Rhodes was once infested with snakes and the deer helped control the population. They have interesting antlers, like a beautiful set of wings, stretching backwards then widening out like fans atop the heads of the males. At the port are statues of a female and male on the two pillars forming the harbor entrance. The male looks about to take flight.

The Palace of the Knights has circular, medieval towers as if plucked from Central Europe, a lovely courtyard, and neat small pyramids of stacked cannonballs.

The remainder of Rhodes Town is eclectic with Venetian buildings, Turkish fountains and mosques, minarets like ornate guided missiles pointing to the heavens ready to launch, and a small synagogue with a huge wooden scroll of the Ten Commandments.

One December when I visited with my parents, brother and sister, we met a young Greek man on the beach while looking across at the barren hills of Turkey, less than thirty miles away. He was returning from swimming, and in hospitable Greek fashion he invited us to his home for a drink. I asked about swimming in

December. He said, "You can do it if you swim all year round. You can't just go out in December and swim."

The center of the island is mountainous and as you drive across the highest ridges, the olive trees have grown and slanted one way, the direction of the prevailing winds. Moving toward the Temple of Athena at Lindos, you pass through "The Valley of the Butterflies," where a carpet of orange "tiger" moths with black stripes cover the ground like marigolds.

The best "travelogue" for the island is the classic, old motion picture "The Guns of Navarone" with a great cast including Gregory Peck, David Niven, then Irene Pappas, Anthony Quinn and James Darren portraying Greeks. You even get to hear Darren sing a lovely Greek folk song. The scenes shot at Lindos and the old city are timeless.

My favorite book about Rhodes is also a classic. "Reflections on a Marine Venus" by the fine Mediterranean travel writer, Lawrence Durrell, set in Rhodes immediately after World War II when Durrell came here after spending the war years in of all places, Alexandria, Egypt. The slim book is another piece of time travel magic. Durrell's "Marine Venus" is a statue discovered at the bottom of Rhodes harbor in 1929. My favorite statue in the museum is another Venus, a small exquisite model of a crouching Aphrodite (Venus) washing her hair. I like it because she is actually doing something, not just being nude. It existed in the time of Jesus.

Lindos town consists of whitewashed buildings snuggling around the base of a hill upon which sits a 14th century Crusaders' fort and on the very top of the hill, the ruins of the Temple of Athena. The bay is an almost perfect circle opening to the open sea, the beach peppered with bathers. Lindos can be blazing hot in midsummer on the sheltered, southeast side of the island.

Ephesus

Within two days Philo and Yeshua headed toward Athens. Philo decided to bypass Pergamon. It was a bit out of the way and he heard they had little for sale. Another reason: a nearby city had eclipsed Pergamon as the capital of Rome's province in Asia.

It was a quick voyage from Rhodes to blossoming Ephesus on the coast of Asia Minor. A short canal linked the sea to the city. It was developing both as the capital and a prosperous commercial port. The *agora* buzzed. Stalls with fruits, vegetables, meat, fish, clothing and wares. And what the two men desired, the booksellers.

"Yeshua, let us split up. See what we can find."

He nodded and began to look through the scrolls. As he thumbed through parchments at an obscure stand, something caught his eye. He picked up a scroll and unwound the bottom portion. A signature was scrawled at the bottom, *"Nausiphanes."* He unwound the top of the scroll; his eyes widened. He replaced the document in the barrel and walked to Philo.

"Rabbi, I may have found something." Philo followed as Yeshua retraced his steps. The younger man pulled out the manuscript and said, "Take a look at the title and author." The older man's jaw dropped and he said, "Keep looking." Philo took the document and began haggling with the scroll merchant. Money was exchanged and the document wrapped in another parchment.

The rabbi strode to his assistant. "Keen eye, Yeshua. This could be worth our entire trip."

"It could be a fake."

"For what I paid it is worth the gamble. Come, let us go to our inn."

When they entered their room Philo spread the scroll on the table and used small paper weights to hold the edges. The title was simply 'On Ethics.' "Obviously Yeshua, you know something of Nausiphanes. What have you heard?"

"Student of Democritus, teacher of Epicurus until they had some sort of falling out."

"Correct. Now, if this document is authentic and if it echoes, or better yet states the ethical teachings of Democritus, why is that important?"

"Little of his ethical theory and philosophy are documented. Fragments only. Of his scientific philosophies and theories, much more is known."

"Again correct. My colleagues back in Alexandria will establish authenticity. Now what else seems to fit concerning this scroll?"

"Geography. Ephesus is near the areas where Nausiphanes and Epicurus lived, the island of Samos,

Teos, Colophon, the island of Lesbos, and not far from the home of Democritus in Thrace."

Philo stared at Yeshua. "You never cease to amaze me. For someone whose primary interest is Hebrew scriptures, your knowledge of Greek philosophy and history is impressive. You have been reading at night."

Yeshua nodded, still looking at the manuscript. "Well, to some degree I also had access in Sepphoris."

"Let us celebrate your find, my young friend. It becomes warm outside. I suggest after a rest, we visit one of the local *tavernas.*"

Their inn was a short distance from the commercial *agora* near the Great Theater of Ephesus, one of the largest in the Mediterranean world. As afternoon faded and the sunshine lost strength Philo began to stir from his nap. Yeshua was on the balcony with a cool cup of water, gazing at the city and the port to the west. Above the harbor the brush of the fading sun painted the clouds different shades of rose and blue, constantly changing color, shape and position like a slow-motion moving picture. They sat and enjoyed the cooling afternoon.

"Yeshua, are you hungry?"

"Yes."

"Good, let us find a place. What are you hungry for?

"How about lamb?"

"Fine."

They walked toward the harbor, boats gently bobbing at anchor like slender multi-colored corks. A *taverna* with a good view advertised both lamb and fish. "Yeshua?"

"Looks perfect."

They sat and ordered.

As they gazed at the port in the now setting sun Philo said, "A fascinating thing to me is the similarity between the ethical teachings of Democritus and Epicurus. Philosophers like to tease out differences and analyze them. I have always been more interested in seeing where they run parallel. How they harmonize and integrate. Both brilliant men, but I believe Democritus was the truly original thinker. Epicurus was the more charismatic and diplomatic leader, and it is proven in how his ethics are enduring ... and changing very little over time.

"Unlike the schools of the Cynics and Stoics and others."

"Precisely. Those teachings are tending to evolve but Epicurean thought is holding quite firm. Epicurus was practical in having good structure to his overall philosophy. A generous man, opening his school "The Garden" in Athens even to women and slaves, sharing his food. An extrovert and a genius, which is rare. I believe he copied much more from Democritus than he would admit."

The next morning they returned to the commercial *agora*, searching for more manuscripts. Philo made a few purchases, nothing compared to Yeshua's discovery the day before.

*****

When I visited Ephesus, we landed at Kusadasi on the coast. Because of river silting the ruins are even further from the sea than in the first century. Kusadasi offers fine colorful, woven Turkish rugs. It is easy to envision flying one of these "magic carpets" in from Baghdad.

Our tour took us to the ruins. I don't like to use that word for Ephesus. To me it's the most extensive "remains" of any Mediterranean city from ancient times. The amphitheater expanded after the time of Jesus to a whopping 24,000 seats and a stage added because this was now the Roman era. Still used today for concerts by well-known international stars.

You can tell a Greek theater from a purely Roman one because Greeks built their theaters into the side of a hill while Roman ones tended to be free-standing. The engineering became better "through time."

About a century after Jesus a Great Library was built near the center of town, the most impressive ancient library remains I have seen anywhere. The interior is nicely restored, but the facade is stunning. Two stories high with three entrances on the first floor and three openings on the second.

There are eight Corinthian columns on the ground floor and six functional columns on the upper floor. Each of the first floor columns are paired about six feet apart and connected with a capstone laying across the tops. This makes four pairs of columns. Three pairs of columns on the second floor are supported by the first floor but they are offset. Moving right to left, the first left column on the ground floor supports the first right column on the second floor. The second right column on the first floor supports the first left column on the top floor. They straddle one another like a pyramid of cheerleaders at a college football game with the upper cheerleaders standing with a leg on one shoulder of the lower cheerleaders and the other leg on the nearest shoulder of the next cheerleader. So it continues across this marvelous facade of tall columns of marbled stone. The pillars in the middle of the structure are a bit taller than the ones toward the outside. This gives the illusion the library is taller than it really is.

To the right of the Library is the Gate of Augustus (built in honor of the emperor) which leads down a street to the amphitheater. Nearby is an excavated slab the tour guides enjoy pointing out. It always gets attention. It is an ancient advertisement for the local brothel. There is an image of a woman with a bulging money purse beside her. Before her is a crosshatch indicating an intersection (directions). To her left is the outline of a "*large* foot." Men only! Above the foot is a picture of a heart.

Ephesus was prominent in early Christianity. The apostle Paul visited here and a church established. Paul's letter to the Ephesians is an important epistle. It is said the apostle John also lived here, possibly taking care of Mary the mother of Jesus. Timothy, to whom

Paul wrote two New Testament letters was the first bishop of Ephesus.

*****

Within a day Yeshua and Philo were aboard a ship, headed west to Athens. They passed the island of Patmos with its numerous fine beaches and bays. The island is shaped like a great seahorse, gazing toward the coast of the mainland.

Patmos was not prominent in the time of Jesus, but things soon got going. It was an island of exiles and other "offenders," the apostle John banished on it for some time. Here he wrote the Revelation of Jesus Christ, the last book in the New Testament and the only apocalyptic one. It is prophetic, visionary and full of images, which have been interpreted in various ways. They say John wrote it in a cave during his short exile on Patmos. When I visited the traditional cavern I observed the "triple crack" through which God spoke to John as he wrote the Revelation. The cave today is developed, a pilgrimage site for visits by many Christian tourists.

Patmos had its ups and downs through history, harried by pirates, but what really cemented it as a major Christian site was when in 1088, Alexis Comnenus ascended the Byzantine throne. He awarded the island to one of his pious supporters who had predicted he would become emperor. This man, Christodoulos founded a monastery on Patmos, financed by the emperor. Christodoulos also received sea trade rights and tax exemptions.

Over the following centuries, the monastery withstood pirates. Then came nominal control by the

Ottomans (who respected the tax-free status), Venetians, Russians and in the 20th century, Italians. In the late 1940s, Patmos joined independent Greece.

There are two main settlements: Skala, the prosperous main port and Chora, a whitewashed village surrounding the venerable monastery. Chora has fine sea captains' homes, which along with the monastery and the remainder of the island reflect its prosperous past and present. The monastery contains valuable documents. Philo and Yeshua would certainly visit today, although I doubt they could acquire any.

*****

On they sailed passing a small barren island like so many in the Aegean, harassed by pirates. The island was Mykonos.

There was no reason for Yeshua and Philo to stop. There was nothing scholarly about the island then, and there isn't now. It was just another island until the mid-1950s. Then celebrities began to arrive and buy homes. They come still, drawn by the perfect example of a Greek island harbor town, whitewashed houses outlined in fine blue, sometimes red lines with five idyllic windmills cresting the hill over the port guarding the town, like a row of stout white-jacketed guards of the same height and build, shaggy brown cone-shaped heads, the circular cloth fans twirling like semaphores in front. Over the hill are houses and cocktail bars plunging vertically into the surging sea. They have the same bright mix of red, white and blue. The area is nicknamed "Little Venice."

The numerous beaches (family, nude or gay) are superb, the streets and shops immaculate. I got happily lost in the maze of streets moving up from the harbor, laid out long ago to confuse pirates and the blustery wind. I have a copper wall hanging painted in rich enamel, depicting buildings, churches and windmills climbing the hill in a perfect semicircle. The entire island of Mykonos has 700 churches: medium, small and midget-size. I sometimes ask guests in my home to count the churches on the copper painting. Some are hard to spot. My friends seldom come up with the correct answer. Odd such a hedonistic island has so many churches, but the local Greeks who serve the tourists are not copycats.

Today Mykonos is "party central." The town is quiet by day, the beaches jammed. At night and into early morning it vibrates and rocks with all the newly scorched, regular tourists who followed the celebrities here.

*****

Their ship sailed on toward Athens, passing Cape Sounion with its Temple of Poseidon at the southeast extreme of the Attic peninsula. At the top of the peninsula, mighty Athens nestles on *seven* great hills, just like Rome. Legend says Theseus, son of King Aegeus, volunteered to foil a tribute being paid by Athens to King Minos of Crete. Every *seven* years, *seven* young men and *seven* young women were sacrificed to the Minotaur, a half-bull/half-man monster living in an underground labyrinth on Crete. There must be something about that number *seven*. With the help of Ariadne, daughter of Minos, Theseus used a cord to trace his steps through the complicated maze. He killed the beast, made his way out and with Ariadne set sail for Athens to reunite with his father. Stopping at the island of Naxos, he was forced to leave her behind.

He had agreed with his father that when he approached Athens, if victorious he would sail a white flag instead of the customary black one. Grief-stricken over Ariadne he forgot to change sails. His father Aegeus waiting at Sounion, saw the black sail, assumed his son killed, then threw himself into the bay and drowned. The Aegean Sea was named for him.

Today the Temple of Poseidon, God of the Sea, looks out from Sounion upon those waters as Aegeus once did.

Their ship moved on, entering the great Saronic Gulf, heading northwest. They approached Athens, the ancient Parthenon crowning one of the prominent hills. Nearing the port of Piraeus, ahead lay the island of Salamis where centuries before a sea battle had changed history. During a Persian-Greek war, things were going badly for the home team. The Greek city-states had allied (rare) to face the threat. The Persians drove the Greeks back at the famous Thermopylae where 300 Spartans fought to the death to buy time for their comrades to retreat to Athens.

At Salamis the united Greek fleet was vastly outnumbered, just like their armies. The large Persian armada made a fatal mistake by entering the narrow strait between Salamis and the mainland with their large fleet and large ships. The Greeks struck. With brilliant tactics and daring movements, they routed the enemy. The balance tipped. The Persians retreated from Greece.

Athens

The ship carrying Yeshua and Philo docked at Piraeus, and they found transport to the Athens *agora* area at the foot of the Acropolis hill on which the Parthenon temple stood. Philo knew the area well and found accommodations at a nearby inn. They rested until evening.

Over dinner at an outdoor table Philo said, "You have a bright future. Someday you will be a chief librarian, maybe even head librarian in Alexandria."

Yeshua nodded.

"You do not seem very excited."

"I do not know what the future holds."

"It is your decision."

"Not entirely."

"Who then?"

"Philo, God speaks through more than scrolls. He speaks through Nature, through the miraculous coincidences and events of life, through the heart and intuition, ... through the Spirit."

"You hear this voice?"

"In a way."

"Yeshua, you are blessed of God. Most people have few or no choices in life. You not only have remarkable abilities and learning. Your family has means."

"I am very grateful for all that."

"Let us talk of other things. How is your food?"

"The fish is wonderful." He looked at the lemon wedges on the edge of his plate. "Do the Greeks squeeze lemon juice on everything?"

"Nearly everything. Perhaps that is one reason they are so healthy."

"And this wine. It has a pine-like flavor."

"Yes, pine resin. The wine is *retsina*. You will only find it in Greece."

Next morning they set out for the *agora* and climbed a small hill heading south from their inn. There it was, the great marketplace stretching before them, a flurry of activity already. Merchants, food-sellers, groups of men talking with arms waving, entertainers working for a donation. To the left of the *agora* the Parthenon rose like a great phoenix on a large mini-mesa in the brilliant morning sun. Right at the edge of the market, a large temple sat on a smaller hill. Similar in design to the Parthenon, not as grand.

Philo said, "There is the Temple of Hephaestus. Considering your background, you must know something of him."

"Yes, the Greek god of craftsmen. I am more interested in the craftsmanship. Doric style architecture, most easily recognized by the tops of the columns. Rounded tops with square capstones, the columns widening a bit all the way down until they rest directly on the floor of the structure. No base. Originally quite squat like the temple of Apollo at Corinth. These are elongated and quite attractive in their own way. It is said the design originated in Doria, western Greece."

"Yeshua, I am anxious to see what manuscripts might be for sale."

"Go ahead, I will catch up. I want to study the temple."

After a time he rejoined Philo. "How does it look?"

"Better than I hoped. It stands to reason. There is no great library in Athens now. It was destroyed several centuries ago; it seems natural to find so many scrolls in the market. Go, start at the far end and work your way back to me."

They worked into early afternoon, poring over the documents. Philo walked to the younger man. "I have had enough for one day."

"Will we return tomorrow?"

"Yes."

"Good, I want to see the Parthenon."

"We could do that tomorrow morning or even later this evening. The sky looks clear."

They returned to the inn, ate a mid-day meal, then rested. When they arose it was still quite light.

Philo said, "I feel all right Yeshua. Would you like to visit the Parthenon now?"

"Fine."

They walked through the *agora* and veered left to the base of the Acropolis hill. Then rented two donkeys for the climb. They tethered the animals at the top and passed through the ornate entrance to the summit. The entry consisted of three smaller structures, each fine pieces in their own right.

And there it was, basking in the liquid Greek sunshine, like no other. Crystal clear light that wraps around objects and makes them so distinct you feel you have just awoken from a dream into the real world. At first you cannot figure out what makes the Parthenon so stunning. Other temples are just as large, maybe larger. Maybe it's the setting. Maybe it's the type of marble. Maybe it's a combination plus other things no mortal can discern.

It is a temple. A temple to what?

Yeshua and Philo roamed all over the structure. Inside, outside, from a distance, from different vantage points. They withdrew a bit, sat and gazed.

Philo asked, "Did the temple meet your expectations?"

"More than met."

"Some say it is a temple to Athena, the goddess of the city. Some say to the concept of democracy. Others say wisdom, the human spirit, the vision of Pericles. What do you say?"

Yeshua said, "To me it is a temple to Nature, and Nature is the shadow of God. The designers and builders were inspired. A good craftsman is precise. These designers were precise, but not in the normal way. Almost nothing is built in a direct line although that is the illusion. It is like this in Nature. Most things have a curve. The base of the entire structure is slightly domed, not flat. The same with the roof. It gives a feeling of upward movement to the entire building. All the columns slant slightly inward. There is no feeling of weight or strain, rather a type of buoyancy. The corner columns are a bit taller and thicker than the others, again giving an uplifting feeling to the structure. Those four corner columns point diagonally inward toward their opposite corner. If they continued up into the sky, all four columns would eventually meet. A precise Doric column tapers gradually thicker as it drops to its base. These columns are slightly wider in the center, which actually makes them seem more uniform, not as thin."

"Very little in God's creation is exactly straight, and little in the Parthenon is, although we tend to think so at first glance. There is a reflection of real life in this temple. As I said, these designers were inspired. Great engineers and excellent students of Nature."

The older man listened when Yeshua went into one of his discourses. There was a story-like quality to them. Always concise, mentally organized, leading to a point or conclusion. They were too short to be true allegories. Too long for a simple metaphor. Something unique and in-between.

Philo said, "The sun is ebbing. We should get those donkeys down the hill while they can still see their hooves."

*****

The inn where Yeshua and Philo stayed was in a residential area. In our time it became known as the "Plaka" and evolved into a lively section of restaurants, bars and *bouzouki* music clubs, one of the nighttime hot spots in Athens. The ancient marketplace migrated the same direction. Today in its modern form, it's known as the Monastiraki (little monastery) area of the city, named after a small church in the square. Boutiques, specialty shops, souvenirs, old things and new, a flea market atmosphere every day. The ancient *agora* is now a deserted, but well preserved site.

I grew up in a small coal-mining and railroad town, perched on the highest ridge of the Appalachian Mountains in western Pennsylvania. It lay between the cities of Altoona and Johnstown. One summer evening my Greek girlfriend (who became my wife) and I strolled around Monastiraki, and I noticed two older women leaving a restaurant, speaking English amidst a torrent of otherwise Greek tongues. I listened to their accent for a moment, then said to Vasso, "Those two women are from my home area."

"Really?"

I approached the two ladies and asked, "Where are you from?"

With a startled look when she heard English, one woman replied, "We're from Pennsylvania."

"I know you're from Pennsylvania. Where in Pennsylvania?"

"Well, I'm from Johnstown," and glancing at the other lady she said, "and my friend is from Altoona."

We ended up at their fine hotel, the Royal Olympic, listening to a grand piano in the lobby. I believe they were thrilled to be chatting with a "hometown boy" and his Greek girlfriend.

In the modern marketplace of Monastiraki you can find most anything, old or new. During my time in Greece, *flocati* rugs were popular. The Greek *flocati* sheep do not have curly wool. Theirs is long and straight and it comes in pointed narrow bunches, several inches long like thin, white, sharpened pencils. As if you skinned a sheep and its braids of hair sprout from that woven carpet as they had from the animal's hide. *Flocatis* make fine, decorative, pure-white throw rugs.

When I lived in Athens I would visit the market on Saturday mornings and stroll the narrow streets lined with shops. I became friendly with one young merchant named Niko who sold *flocatis*. We chatted every time I went his way.

I left Greece when my Air Force assignment finished. Vasso and I went to America and were married. It was five years until I again visited Greece. I made my way to Monastiraki, wondering if I would see my friend again. Perhaps he no longer worked there.

Perhaps we weren't really friends. Maybe I was simply a customer among the hundreds he saw all the time. I walked down his lane, and there he was. A little heavier, outside at the street-side display, talking with a customer. When I was about twenty meters away, he glanced in my direction, our eyes locked and a big smile crossed his face.

"Davi !!"

Big bear hug, back slapping. We talked as if a day hadn't gone by. I was home.

I loved watching meat (typically pork) being sliced from a revolving vertical spit in some of the restaurants. Often the rotisserie was next to the sidewalk so potential patrons could watch the show. The heated burner was on one side, the meat sliced off the open side. The sandwiches and meat made with pita bread are known as *gyros*. Pronounced "ye-row." Think of *gyro*-scope. Spinning meat.

Crete

The two librarians spent another day in the *agora* until Philo felt satisfied. They booked passage for Alexandria and left the following day. Their ship sailed south toward the largest Greek island, Crete. The boat headed for Gortyna on the southern coast, then it would continue to Alexandria.

The winds were favorable, from the north this time of year, and they made good time. Their craft skirted the west coast of Crete. East along the northern coast was Cydonia (modern day Hania) then further east the great Knossos. They turned left along the southern coast of the big island, bound for Kali Limenes (Fair Havens), the main port for Gortyna. Forty years later, the apostle Paul would be blown off course to this very spot on his way to Rome.

Gortyna had prospered under Roman rule as the favored Cretan city. After their ship docked, Yeshua and Philo strolled the beach.

"I did not expect to see bananas growing here. They are much smaller than our Egyptian ones," said the younger man.

"This may be as far north as they grow. I have never seen them anywhere else in Greece."

They would sleep on board tonight as the ship was scheduled to leave at dawn. They found a seaside *taverna,* and as they ate, Yeshua asked, "Philo, what do you think of the Greek religious ideas?"

"Well, I am Hebrew, as you are. I believe in our revelation. Polytheism never made much sense to me. How about you?"

"Very much the same. But, your work is a study of comparisons and parallels between Greek and Hebrew thought."

Philo said, "Too many people of every faith become very rigid about their beliefs. God is not small. His revelation to other people may be different. To shrink God to our size never seemed intelligent to me."

At dawn the next day the crew moved, getting ready to cast off. Yeshua and Philo came topside with steaming cups of tea. The young man said, "The sky looks favorable."

"As many voyages as you made to Palestine, you should know."

*****

I arrived in Crete via an Olympic Airways flight from Athens. The pilot must have been a burnt-out former Greek air force aviator, the way he dove steeply for the runway and banked hard reminded me of my academy days in the backseat of fighter planes. But we landed safely.

Crete is 120 miles long and twenty to forty miles wide, shaped like a ship sailing east with steering mechanism in the rear, a fin in the center of the keel on the underside and an uplifted bow in the front. Very appropriate for Greece. The capital of Crete, Iraklion is a hodgepodge as is Cretan history. Over the centuries the Romans, Byzantines, Arabs, Venetians and Turks all had a go at ruling the island, never the spirit of the people.

Turkish fountains, a Venetian harbor and Loggia (balcony), Roman sculptures in the museum, Byzantine churches and monastery nearby, Crete never achieved true independence until 1898. Fifteen years later it joined Greece.

The most inspiring ruin on Crete is Knossos, just southeast of Iraklion. This was the capital of the ancient Minoan civilization. It flourished from 2000 to 1000 B.C. They were great merchants and seamen, trading with the Greek mainland and islands, and as far as

Egypt. The palace of Knossos had great pillars, the opposite of Doric. The Minoan columns were wider at the top than the bottom. They were reconstructed for the palace ruins and are fire-red in color. Many of the interior walls are red, some human figures shown on the walls are a bronzed-red. There are even red fish pictured on the walls, swimming among dolphins.

This was a feminine culture, the bull revered. There is a wonderful image of a bronzed female vaulting over a bull.

The water drainage system at Knossos is as good as modern day Athens, maybe better. And we think we've advanced.

When I left Knossos somehow I found myself in a potato field, and I couldn't escape that vibrant color. The dirt was red, the vegetable bags were red mesh, the smiling faces of the workers were red from the sun. As the sun set the clouds glowed rose-color.

In the same area is the mountain village of Anogeia. A center of revolution and resistance. The village was burnt to the ground at least twice. Once by the Turks. Then during WWII British and Greek commandos captured a German general in this area and extradited him to Egypt. The Cretans paid for this. Once again Anogeia was burnt. Hitler used his elite paratroop corps to invade the island. They did it without naval backup, which was amazing. They took control of Crete, but their losses were so heavy from local resistance Hitler never used his crack paratroops again.

One of the British commandos who helped kidnap the German general was Major Patrick Leigh

Fermor who after the war became known as a fine travel writer, drawing on his wartime experiences as a guerrilla fighter with the local resistance and his earlier time as a young man walking across Europe to Turkey. He's been called the "real" Indiana Jones.

I drove into the village. Men sat outside a *kafenion,* sipping coffee from cups like golf balls with tiny handles. The locals at one table were an advertisement for "Men in Black." Well-polished high black boots, black trousers, shirts and bandanas. The younger men had great black mustaches. The older men salt and pepper. They all had black stares.

*****

The voyage across the sea was rough but swift with good winds. They pulled into Alexandria by evening the second day, and the two companions walked toward the Library. Philo stopped. "Thank you, my friend. Having you with me was an absolute delight. You need not come to the Library tomorrow."

"Thank you for taking me. Shalom."

"Shalom."

The next morning he and Miriam drank tea in the atrium. Yari was already in the city on business. Yeshua rose. "Thank you for the tea."

"We missed you, son."

"I love you, Aunt." He walked away. Her moist eyes followed him.

He spent time in the gymnasium then walked along the harbor. He was outside Esther's synagogue school when she finished for the day.

"Yeshua!" She ran to him. "When did you get back?"

"Last night."

"And you waited this long to see me?"

"Where are you going?"

"Market."

"I will come."

Esther moved through the market. Everyone greeted her and looked with curious eyes at the tall young man. He carried her purchases.

She finished buying and placed everything in one sack. He took the bag.

"Are you sure it is not too heavy for you?"

"I have already been to the gymnasium."

They strolled along the water. Too soon, they were at her home.

"Will you come in?"

"No, thank you. Shalom."

"Shalom."

He leaned forward, kissed her on the cheek and walked away.

The year moved into autumn and soon it was cool enough for get-togethers at the home of Miriam and Yari. Yeshua sat with Esther's parents. She burst upon them, flushed, eyes wide. "Yeshua, you are not dancing!"

"I leave it to you. You are better than me."

"Now you are telling stories."

"It was a compliment."

"Come on."

"Why would I leave the most attractive woman in your household for second-best?"

Esther punched him lightly in the shoulder. Her mother leaned in. "You are still telling stories."

He walked with the young woman toward the dancing as she grabbed his arm, her face in excited profile, eyes wide, looking up and chattering at Yeshua as he nodded and looked straight ahead.

Her mother looked at her husband. "Who made that one?"

"God knows."

The evening moved on. The music faded and fell along with the light and warmth of the day.

Esther and Yeshua returned to her parents. "Daughter, we must go. Young man, when will you come and dine with us again?"

"Any time, you are a fine cook."

"More stories."

"No, I have this on good authority."

"Who?"

"Your daughter."

"Well, at least she has something good to say about me."

"She says many good things."

"Tell me."

"Do you have an hour?

She said, "Galilean, as much as you try to hide it, you are a very kind person. Shalom."

"Shalom."

Alexandria rolled into winter, just as the waves crashed on the shore, stronger, colder, harder. One day in the Library, Yeshua said, "Philo, Reza of Persia asked me to become his assistant."

"Why do you mention Reza? Every scholar with half-a-brain is asking for you."

"I told him I will not leave you."

"Of course you did, but why do you bring up his name?"

"I am interested in Eastern religion and philosophy."

"Greek and Hebrew are not enough?"

"No."

"Reza is a good man. I will speak with him."

Two days later Philo said, "Yeshua, I spoke with Reza. You will work half a day with me, half a day with Reza."

"That is not fair to you."

"Let me determine what is fair. I would rather have you half a day than anyone else for a full day. It is settled."

Yeshua began work in the afternoons with the Persian scholar.

Several days later Yeshua was at Esther's home for evening meal. As they sat, Esther's father asked, "Young man, will you give the blessing?"

He rose from the table. A passage from the Torah came from his lips. It started in his heart, rose through his chest like a surging river, cascading through the room and beyond. It crested and fell, but never ceased moving on. Rising to the rafters, flowing through the walls. The buzz from nearby houses died. Everyone listened as the ancient verses seemed to make the walls quiver. At last it rose to the heavens, then fell ... to calm and silence.

All was still. Esther's mother said, "Yeshua, is there anything you cannot do?"

Esther's father said, "He cannot find a wife."

Everyone went silent. Esther blushed and looked at the floor. Yeshua gazed at the older man. Esther's mother glared at her husband. "Nathan!"

"I said what I had to say. I will not say it again. More wine, Yeshua?"

He held out his goblet as the older man poured.

Esther looked up and met Yeshua's eyes. He smiled. Her redness faded.

Fires burned in homes, extra blankets on beds, the days began to lengthen in light. Slow at first, then more and more. Harvesting of lemons finished. Summer trees budded.

As Spring wakened a dormant world, Yeshua walked into Philo's office.

"Reza is making a journey to Babylon."

"So?"

"He asked me to go."

Philo put down his quill and leaned back. "Please, sit down."

"Do you want to go?"

"Yes."

Philo spread his fingers, pointed them upwards, the rights ones touching the left. He peered over his little spire. "Will you convert to the Babylonian mysteries?"

Yeshua smiled.

"How about Zoroastrianism? They believe in one God ... I think you should go."

The younger man's face went blank.

"What is the matter?"

"I expected more resistance."

"No, it will be good for you. When Alexander the Great conquered Babylon three hundred years ago, he respected and preserved the city. After his death his heirs fell to squabbling and the city went into decline. People moved away, but over time many returned. The city is functioning now, the Persians are in control and the library has survived well. It remains a place of learning and faded grandeur. The region is stable. The library is intact, and it is very good. Babylon was always a center of learning. Who knows? Perhaps you will be able to pry some good manuscripts from those characters. I will never make such a trip."

Yeshua grinned ear to ear.

"What makes you so happy? There is one person who will not like this at all. What will you tell her?"

"That I will return."

Philo let out a long breath. "You are the most gifted person I have ever known, but your attitude towards women amazes me."

Esther was in a rage. "You are going *where*?!"

"Babylon."

"How long will you be gone?"

"Several months, maybe more."

"What will I do?"

"You have your school, your family, I understand your older brothers are beginning to have children ..."

"What will I do without you?"

He was silent.

"Oh Yeshua, you have the answers to so many things, but you do not have the answer to that ... besides what will I do if you are enticed by some Persian girl?"

He held back a smile. When Esther began to tease him, he knew he had won.

"I hear they are attractive."

She pushed him so hard he almost lost his balance.

In two weeks he and Reza were ready and on the dock in the morning. Philo, Yari, Miriam, Esther and her parents were there. Yeshua said his goodbyes. Esther was last.

"I spend too much time on this dock saying goodbye to you."

"I always return, ... and I will this time."

They embraced. The ship cast off.

Again docking at Caesarea Maritima, Yeshua spent a short time with his friends, then he and Reza joined a caravan bound for Babylon. At dawn the caravan headed northeast for Damascus. They passed the Sea of Galilee, through the pass north of today's Golan Heights, and by sundown the third day they pulled into a caravan stop east of Damascus.

As they sat around the fire at evening, Yeshua spoke. "Reza, I assume you are anxious to be home."

"Of course, it has been some years."

"I am sure you could get a good position at the Library of Babylon."

"It is tempting, but mine is a troubled land. In Alexandria there is stability and it is one of the great libraries of our world, perhaps the greatest."

"You sound like me. My land is troubled also."

"Of course."

The next day was a long, dry journey, across the desert heading for the nearest bend of the great Euphrates River at Al Bukamal. They arrived as the sun set and made camp.

Relaxing around the fire after evening meal, Reza said, "The difficult part is over, my young friend. Now we follow the river southeast toward Baghdad, then on to Babylon. Water is the life of the earth, as blood is the life of man. Let us rest."

They struck out at dawn, traveling the upper side of the Euphrates. Baghdad was actually on the banks of the Tigris River, which paralleled the Euphrates. In the area of Baghdad and nearby Babylon the rivers nearly touched, Baghdad on the west side of the Tigris, Babylon a bit further on, straddling the banks of the Euphrates.

Babylon

They still had daylight, so they pushed to the outskirts of Babylon and made camp. The next morning broke bright and clear. They sold their camels back to the caravan leader and hired a donkey-driver to carry their belongings into town.

They went to the Library and Reza spoke to the attendant. "I am Reza of the Library of Alexandria. We have an appointment with your head librarian." The young man nodded and disappeared. He returned and ushered them to the head librarian's office. Reza entered and made arrangements. Within a short time he came back.

"Yeshua, they have rooms for both of us. I will probably use mine some nights, as I also have family in town. This man will escort you to your quarters. I will see you tomorrow morning."

The young man beckoned, helped with the baggage and showed Yeshua to a small room in the dormitory. He explained the dining arrangements and departed.

After arranging his belongings, Yeshua left the room and asked the first attendant, "Where may I find the astrologers?"

"This direction, turn right."

He came to a row of offices, found the name he was looking for, knocked on the door.

"Come."

He entered. "Melchior?"

An old man at his writing desk looked up. "Do I know you, young man?"

"Yes, you know me, but I do not know you."

The man squinted. "What does that mean?"

"Over twenty years ago you visited me. I was a child."

"I saw many children twenty years ago."

"You saw me far away in Palestine, in a village named Bethlehem."

The man's eyes and mouth grew large. He stood. "No."

"You and two companions gave me gifts. Gold, frankincense, myrrh. Yours was gold."

He ran around the desk like a boy, grabbed the young man's hands and kissed them. "Lord Yeshua, I cannot believe it. What are you doing here?"

He explained.

"I know Reza, good man. Where do you stay?"

"They gave me a room here."

"Bah! This place is like an army barracks, and the food is wretched. You must come and stay with me. I have a large home on the river. Cool evening breezes, plenty of space. Our children have grown and gone away. My wife will be thrilled, she is a fine cook, and she does not get much practice now. I eat little."

"Thank you, I will think about it."

"Think! There is no thinking! But go ahead, take your time. Are you hungry?"

"Actually, yes.

"Good, let us go. I know a place on the river."

They sat at a restaurant, the thick green river oozing by. Melchior said, "Lord Yeshua, tell me everything, your life, from the beginning; I am a good listener."

The young man began and took his time. Food came. The story continued. At last he stopped.

"And what brought you here, Yeshua?"

"I want to learn the Eastern ways. Your beliefs, your way of life ... your spirituality."

"Alexandria with its Hebrew and Greek are not sufficient?

"The same thing my librarian said."

"Reza?"

"No, I work with Philo of Alexandria. I am rather on loan to Reza."

"Your librarian is broad-minded. I have heard of Philo. Hebrew. Makes sense."

Within three days Yeshua had relocated to Melchior's ample home within the city walls on the east bank of the Euphrates. After evening meal they sat on the veranda, watching the setting sun. Melchior's wife, Aliyah joined them.

"Madam, your husband told the truth. The food was wonderful."

The routine began. One afternoon Yeshua sat at his desk near Reza. The Persian asked, "What are you doing here?"

"The day is not over."

"It is for you. I have you half a day in Alexandria by Philo's generosity. The same here. You work the mornings."

Yeshua rose. "Thank you." The older man nodded.

He walked out of the library and turned left. The gymnasium was just ahead. He went in and found his way to the wrestling area. Several young men saw him enter.

"Who is he?"

"Never saw him."

"Let us have some fun with him." They walked his direction.

"Hello, stranger."

"Hello."

"You have an accent."

"So do you."

They laughed. One stepped forward. "My name is Farad. You are a wrestler?"

"I have wrestled."

"Would you like to give it a try?"

"Sure. Let me get rid of some of these clothes and warm up." Yeshua stripped off his outer garments and spent about five minutes limbering.

He returned to the three Persians.

"I am ready."

Farad pointed. "The mat over there."

They squared off and began to circle. One of the other Persians said, "This will not take long."

The Persian lunged for a grab. Yeshua side-stepped him. More circling, another move. The Hebrew jumped aside. "Come on stranger, engage!"

The Babylonian's eyes grew hot. He charged again, Yeshua pushed him down and was on top. The Persian strained left, then right under the strong grip, searching for weakness. He rolled and came out above. Yeshua was face down on the mat. Back and forth they pushed and squeezed, muscles bulging.

This went on for three periods. Yeshua was now underneath and the local man worked to leverage him over. He pushed hard to the right, too hard. The Hebrew flipped him on his back and pinned him to the mat. The referee's hand slapped the floor. It was over. The other two Persians stood with mouths open.

Farad jumped up. "You provoked me, foreigner!"

Yeshua smiled. "You provoked yourself. I only helped. Perhaps I will not be so fortunate next time."

"What makes you think there will be a next time?"

"I see it in your eyes." He turned to walk away.

"What is your name?"

"Yeshua."

"See you tomorrow."

"Probably not. My bones are cracking."

For the first time Farad smiled.

At this time the city of Babylon was laid out in a rectangle with a double wall and a moat surrounding it. The Euphrates River split it in two, north to south. The walls had nine gates, the city nine temples. There was also a tall *ziggurat,* the *Entemenanki,* which hearkened back to the legend of the Tower of Babel. The *ziggurat* had a temple on the top floor to bring it closer to God. There were gates in the walls of the city in every direction, north, south, east and west.

The nine temples and the *ziggurat* represented the pantheon of Persian gods and goddesses. Over time Marduk rose to chief of the gods. Lesser deities stood for love and sex, war, justice, political power, hunting, the sun, storms, learning, the harvest and so on. It was quite a menu.

The next afternoon Yeshua was in a market near the Library, buying some vegetables to surprise Aliyah. As he looked over the eggplants, a soft voice said, "The vegetables in the rear are better quality."

He looked up. A young woman was on the other side of the table, choosing some eggplants for herself. "They move the older vegetables forward, fresh ones in the rear."

"Good to know."

He looked again. She was about twenty, jet black hair, skin just a shade darker than his, large black eyes. "I have not seen you before."

"I am new."

"Where do you work?"

"The Library."

Her eyes widened. "My father works in the Library."

"Jasmine!" They were interrupted.

"Jasmine, I have not seen you in weeks. Where have you been?"

Now Yeshua interrupted. ""Hello, Farad."

"Yeshua! I hoped to see you at the gymnasium today."

"My bones are still healing."

"Of course. Jasmine, it was good to see you. I must go. Yeshua, see you soon."

She said, "So you are a librarian and a wrestler. Not common."

"It is what it is. Which way are you headed?"

"South along the river."

"So am I. May we walk a bit?"

"All right. I assumed you would be staying at the Library."

"I have a room there, but I stay with an old friend from the Library."

"Who?"

"An astrologer, Melchior."

She stopped. "Melchior! He is one of my father's best friends!"

"These vegetables are for Aliyah."

"So, you shop for her."

"No, she does not know I am buying these. I must figure some way to pay my rent. They will not take my money."

"You must be special to them."

"Melchior is very special to me."

She stopped again. "This is our home, Yeshua."

"Our home?"

"I live with my parents."

"Lucky them."

She said, "It was good to meet you, Yeshua. Goodbye."

That evening after the meal, they sat on the veranda. Aliyah said, "Thank you for the eggplants. They were excellent."

"I had help picking them out. A young woman I met at the market. Her name is Jasmine. Her father works with Melchior."

Both of them laughed. Melchior said, "Jasmine's father does not work *with* me. He is the Head Librarian, but he is a dear friend. I suspect it will not be long until you meet him."

Two weeks later Melchior said, "Yeshua, in two days there is a party at the home of Mahan, Jasmine's father. Aliyah and I are invited. You, too. Will you come?"

"Certainly, I am honored."

They arrived as the sun said goodbye to the day, passing the baton of light to the moon and stars until dawn. Small torches burned at appropriate places to guide footsteps. A dignified man and woman stood at the entrance, greeting guests. Melchior grabbed his friend's arms. "Thank you for inviting us."

"Do not play games with me. You know you were first on the list."

Aliyah followed, her arm in Yeshua's.

Mahan said, "Aliyah, my dear, is this the young man we have heard about?"

"It depends what you have heard."

"You are Yeshua. Welcome to our home."

"The honor is mine, sir."

They continued, greeting Mahan's wife. Jasmine was next. "Hello, Yeshua."

"Good evening, Jasmine."

Melchior said, "Yeshua, come with us. It is much better on the upper floor." They made their way to a veranda with cooling breezes, looking at emerging stars and a crescent moon, razor-sharp as a curved dagger.

Jasmine appeared. Yeshua stood and made a place for her beside Aliyah. They chatted for some time. Mahan and his wife approached. They grabbed chairs to sit beside their friends.

After a time Mahan said, "Daughter, show Yeshua the house. I hear he is interested in everything. Perhaps Persian architecture will give him something new to think about."

Jasmine and Yeshua rose and she led him away. They roamed through the upper area, then the ground floor. She looked at him, "Is it much different than your world?"

"Actually, no. The embellishments of the homes are different, a different dialect of Aramaic, different clothing, but I find people are much the same everywhere."

"How do you find our gymnasium?"

"Wonderful. Your friend, Farad, is a fine wrestler."

"Yes, I am sure you will learn a great deal from him."

"I have."

"Well, perhaps someday you will defeat him."

"I have always defeated him."

She stopped and stared. "I am sorry. Did I understand you correctly? Farad is the finest wrestler at the gymnasium. He is champion of the city."

"Well, there are other gymnasiums and other cities, and we have only wrestled three times. He could win."

She kept staring. "Yeshua of Alexandria, you must be the most humble person I have ever met."

"Well, you have not met everyone, and I am not falsely humble."

"How long have you known Melchior?"

"We go back a long time, to when I was a child. It is a long story, better left for another time. Tell me about you."

She began to talk. They wandered a long time, the rear garden, the river, the food and drink tables, the upper floor where the four old friends still sat. Aliyah said, "Yeshua, we should go."

Mahan said, "Yes, and I am neglecting my guests. Excuse me."

Melchior, Aliyah, Yeshua and Jasmine walked to the entrance. "Thank you, my two dear friends for coming. And, thank you Yeshua, for a most interesting evening."

"The pleasure was mine."

After the guests left, Jasmine helped her mother and the servants clean up. "Mother, that is one of the more amazing people I have ever met."

"Daughter, I sense there is something quite unusual about his relationship with Melchior. I cannot put my finger on it, but I know Melchior. He is in awe of that young man."

Reza and Yeshua worked on documents one morning, when the older man paused and said, "Yeshua, as always you are a great help with the work. Tell me, what would you like to concentrate on with the Persian studies?"

"The practical side."

"What do you mean?"

"Not the texts and rules or even the writings, but the real way people employ these teachings in their daily lives. How they walk and talk and live and breathe these ways. *I want to know how to do it, then I want to do it ...* not simply how to think about it."

Reza put down his spectacles. "It is impossible to argue with that. Most everyone takes the easy way. *We fill our brains full of facts and ideas when the real purpose and goal should simply be to just live it.*"

"Go ahead, Yeshua, you have my full permission to do just what you want to do. *And when you finish ... teach me.*"

At evening as they sat on the veranda Yeshua said, "Melchior, tell me about the teachings of Zoroaster.

"It is similar to your Hebrew teachings. The one influenced the other. Zoroaster believed in a supreme god of good, Ahura Mazda or Wise Lord who is uncreated. There is an opposing evil force, not as strong as our god. The teaching of Zoroaster is the main monotheistic religion of the east. In the past other deities were also revered, but that is fading. Sometimes in my contemplative moments I wonder if that is the reason three worshippers of one god were led to you."

"How do you practice your religion?"

"We seek to live a good life based upon good deeds and good thoughts. We consider fire and water to be sacred. So we pray with a flame or fire nearby."

"Do you feel the closeness of your god?"

"I believe I feel him sometimes, not always."

Melchior went on talking about various practices, human responsibility and death, but Yeshua had heard what he wanted.

The next morning Yeshua asked Reza, "What is the difference between the ancient beliefs of the Persians and now, after Zoroaster?"

Reza looked up. "We do not know much about those old beliefs, but I do not think the differences are as great as some suppose. The ancients believed in Ahura Mazda, as do the Zoroastrians. Since they were polytheistic, he was chief among the gods, sort of like the Greek Zeus."

"What was the spiritual attitude or life like for those people?"

"It is unclear, but I suspect it was not much different than today."

Yeshua went to the gymnasium that afternoon to clear his brain. He wrestled with some of his Persian friends. Farad came by. "Come on, Hebrew, I feel lucky today."

"No my friend, I am not in the mood. Too much on my brain."

"You think too much."

"No argument there."

As Yeshua walked home the words of Farad rang in his ears. *"You think too much."*

He spoke out loud to himself, *"Perhaps that is it."*

As usual in evening he sat with Melchior sipping wine on the veranda and watched the evening begin. The Persian said, "You are quiet, Yeshua. What are you thinking?"

"I am trying not to think."

Melchior said, "Must be difficult for you."

"It is not easy, but it is simple. What if thinking is really secondary? What if the heart, the soul, the spirit are primary? The mind is a fine instrument, but perhaps we overuse it."

"Are you trying to put the Library out of business? And you and I out of work?"

Yeshua said, "*God is Spirit, and those who worship Him must worship in Spirit and in Truth* ... not in a particular place, ... and not in the mind."

Melchior gazed at the young man without speaking.

Lights sparkled alive in buildings around them as Melchior lit a small torch. Stars appeared above, mushrooming in number as darkness fell thickly, a black cloak wrapping around the city.

Several days later Yeshua was in the market looking at the stalls. A familiar voice asked, "More eggplants?"

"No, Jasmine, not today. Maybe you can help me. I am looking for a wine for Melchior. Something special. Perhaps a little sweet."

"What does he normally drink?"

"A dry white wine. I believe he calls it Shiraz."

"Shiraz is a small place to the southeast, but the vineyards are growing. They make another darker wine with the same grape. It is slightly sweet. It is a little pricey."

"Well, I do not pay rent."

"If they have it, we should find it over there."

They walked to another stall. "Here it is, Yeshua."

"A very unusual bottle. Is there a *jinn** inside?"

She laughed. "You know of those fables?"

"We have them in Hebrew culture, too. Only we keep them in lamps, not bottles."

"There is no *jinn* in this vessel. Those bottles are much more expensive."

"This one costs enough."

"I warned you."

Yeshua paid for his purchase. "Are you going home?"

"Yes. You may walk with me."

"I did not ask."

"You were about to."

* genie

They moved south.

"Yeshua, I do not understand. Shiraz is a white wine, yet the sweet wine you bought, also called Shiraz is dark."

"The grapes are red. If you separate the juice from the skins quickly, you have a clear wine. If you wait and leave them in contact for a time, the juice darkens and the skins give it a different flavor. Of course there is the aging and fermentation process, but that is the basic difference."

"I see. You know, people are talking about you at the Library."

"Strangers arouse interest."

"It is not because you are a newcomer. It is about your abilities."

"Well, besides wrestling, I can also dance."

She laughed again. "Your abilities as a scholar."

"You are correct. I almost forgot. I can also read and write."

They walked, chatting easily, both smiling. Her home appeared.

"I have not heard you laugh before, Jasmine. You have a good laugh. What happened?"

"What happened?"

"To the laugh."

"An old friendship that went away."

"A man."

She stared at him.

"Let go of the friendship. The world needs your laugh."

"And I believe it needs your sense of humor. Goodbye."

"Goodbye."

The next morning Yeshua asked Reza, "Do we have Hindu texts here?"

"Yes, Section 23, and we have a Hindu scholar. His office is in the north end."

In the afternoon Yeshua walked toward the northern part of the Library and found the man's office. He introduced himself and they talked for a time.

"Sir, I am interested in the *practice* of the Hindu faith. History, rules, deities are quite secondary to me. What would you suggest?"

"I will write down some documents you may look over. Also, we have a small place of Hindu worship in the east end of town. Here is the address and the name of our spiritual leader. I know him personally; he is a good man. Tell him I sent you."

"Thank you."

Yeshua spent the next several afternoons pouring over Hindu texts. He found many variations and flexibilities to the belief system. There was a main god, Brahman, but other deities also, sort of a middle area between polytheism and monotheism. Life was a cycle of birth, life, death and sometimes attainment to "blessedness." More often came reincarnation, the chance to live again and improve.

There was real reverence for life, particularly living creatures. And a belief in the immortal soul, part of a great cosmic soul. Yeshua was anxious to visit this local spiritual leader to see how he lived his faith.

That evening he sat with Aliyah and Melchior, enjoying the evening breeze. "My dear host, I have something for you." He handed the old man an oddly shaped package.

Melchior peeled away the covering and his eyes lit up. "Oh, Yeshua, how did you know this was my favorite?"

"I would like to claim it was intuition, but I had some help."

"Let me guess, female help?"

The young man glanced at Aliyah. "Female help is the best kind."

Melchior said, "We must try it. My dear, would you be kind enough to bring us three goblets?"

Later after Aliyah retired, the old man asked, "How long will you stay with us?"

"I do not know."

"Yeshua, you are like a son I revere. You have given us much happiness in just a few months. Our daughters are gone. They married well; they have fine homes. The husbands have good occupations. We do not see them much. You may stay here as long as you wish. When my wife and I pass, this house is yours."

The Hebrew blinked and looked down. "I have too many homes. Palestine, Alexandria, now Babylon. I do not know what God has for me, but I feel his presence, more and more every day."

Melchior reached and poured a bit more wine for both of them.

The next afternoon Yeshua made his way to the east part of the city and found the small Hindu place of worship. A residence adjoined it. He knocked on the door; an older man opened it.

"My name is Yeshua. I am looking for Amas."

"I am Amas."

"I work at the Library. Your Hindu scholar suggested I speak with you."

"What do you want?"

"I want to know about your beliefs."

"Would you like some tea?"

"Yes." He followed Amas inside and sat at a table while the older man brewed an herbal mix. In a few minutes he returned with a pot and two cups.

Amas spoke of the tenets and principles of the Hindu faith. After some time Yeshua said, "I have read these things. I want to know how you realize the presence of God."

The old man sat back. "The sense of God's presence comes and goes."

"Is there anything in particular you do before it comes."

"No, sometimes it comes during prayer, sometimes when I read the Vedas, sometimes during our gatherings ... sometimes not."

Yeshua looked at him. *"The wind blows where it wishes, and you hear the sound of it, but you do not know where it comes from or where it is going."*

"Yes! That is it. Well said."

They spoke more, back and forth, another cup of tea. Yeshua said, "Thank you for your time. I must go." They walked to the entrance, said their goodbyes.

When he neared Melchior's home, on the western horizon the sun was a large orange, fiery ball, increasing in size, shrinking in warmth. As he entered the house, it hung just above the ridge. Yeshua greeted Aliyah, then went up to the veranda. Melchior sat watching the sun, now half-submerged in the earth, sinking fast.

"Well, young scholar, did those Hindus have better luck converting you than I have?"

"They were no more successful. Good people, though."

Yeshua spread a nearby blanket around the old man's shoulders as Melchior handed him a goblet. "Fair trade."

"Mahan and his wife will have another party the middle of next week. Are you interested?"

"Certainly."

A week later they approached the house, Melchior leading, Yeshua had Aliyah's arm. They made their greetings, moved inside and the Hebrew's eyes widened.

"Excuse me, Madam." He raised his hand. "Farad! What are you doing here?"

"Jasmine asked me."

"Good. Let us get something to eat." They invaded the food tables, then sat.

"Yeshua, what do you think of our girl, Jasmine?"

"She is a fine woman. You should marry her."

"I have tried."

"Of course you have, you have brains and good sense."

"She had a bad experience ..."

"Stop! I know."

"She told you!?"

"No, she said just a few words; I realized what happened."

"That canal rat! You do not treat ..."

"Stop! It is God's blessing. She gets rid of a bad person, then she gets the chance for a good man like you. Be patient."

"Is this the way you live, Hebrew? You see the good in everything?"

"*All things work together for good,* Farad. If we do not see the good, we miss the hand of God every day. I do have a suggestion."

"What?"

"Do not wrestle her. She might beat you."

"Ahhh!" The Persian grabbed him around the shoulders and pretended to squeeze.

A familiar voice said, "Are you two fighting? Who is winning?"

"Farad."

"Give me a seat between you. My home is not a gymnasium."

They moved sideways; she sat. The music started, a folk dance.

"Librarian, once you told me you could dance."

"Not Persian."

"Good, Farad and I will teach you. Come."

She grabbed one hand; Farad clutched the other. Soon they were in the circle, Yeshua watched and imitated the footwork.

When it finished, they retrieved their seats. Farad said, "I need some orange drink. How about you two?" They nodded. He moved away.

"He is a good man, Jasmine. I told him he should marry you."

"You have what we call in Persia a big nose."

"We have the same expression in Palestine. Egypt too, I think. I have two friends, and I want to see them happy."

Farad returned with three drinks. They sipped. The dancing ceased. The musician started to strum with a different rhythm. A man on the far side of the room began a lament in long words that extended forever without cracking. Up, then down. Soft, then louder. It ceased. Several hands clapped.

The long, thin instrument now plucked harsh, twangy sounds offset by melodious voices as one, then another singer took over the changing lyrics. The strings stopped. All quiet.

Yeshua opened his mouth and a soft Persian love song flowed out. The sound circled both sides of the room. Jasmine and Farad looked at each other, then back at their friend. This was no Hebrew chant. More emotional, more variation.

Up on the veranda, conversation stopped. Mahan's wife said, "What is that?"

Melchior stood. "I know that voice." He walked away. The other three followed.

Melchior stood at the ground floor room. The others behind him.

Yeshua took them down a shining river at midday, far out into the burning desert, under palms at sunset, to tents on a moonlit night. Camels moved in shadowy rhythm. Then from a high crescendo, he brought them down a long sandy slope to the embers of a nighttime fire until it slowly died.

Melchior walked away.

Farad began to clap slowly. Others joined in. Soon light applause filled the room. Jasmine put her arm on Farad's shoulder, then leaned over and kissed Yeshua on the cheek.

Farad said, "You lie, Yeshua. You are not Hebrew; you are Persian."

Yeshua rose. "I neglect the others." He walked upstairs, entered the veranda and took a seat. No one said a word. Melchior asked, "Yeshua, some wine? Mahan has Shiraz." The young man looked up, nodded.

The next morning he was again with Reza. "Where will you travel this week, young man? What major religion will you visit?"

"I am thinking of Buddhism, but it seems more philosophy than religion. What do you think?"

"I agree. Buddha was a man who never claimed to be God. He discarded the idea of anyone worshipping him. I find it admirable, but his followers ignored that and created a religion around him, which happens. It seems a good ethical system and appears gaining strength. It grew out of the Hindu faith so it has the idea of reincarnation. The cycle goes on. They say if you advance to "enlightenment," then you escape the cycle and enter some sort of oneness with the Creator. In the past most of those systems were polytheistic, but like our beliefs from Zoroaster, many are moving to an idea of a chief god or one god. Perhaps we have you Hebrews to thank."

"Maybe we do not have so much influence. We are a small group."

"But you are quite firm in your beliefs."

"Some would say stubborn."

Reza said, "You will find the Buddhist scrolls in Section 28 or 29."

Yeshua spent that afternoon with Buddhist documents. He was intrigued. He came back every afternoon for some days until he needed exercise. Then he went to the gymnasium. His friends were excited. "Hebrew, where have you been? Wrestling with your books?"

"Exactly. And I am tired of them. I would rather wrestle with you."

"Bravo! Now you are making sense."

Farad approached. "Come on, my friend, let me limber you up."

"Thank you. I need it."

They worked out easily. After a while, Farad said, "Wait. Let me work on your neck and back muscles. You are tight as a new bow. Lie down on your stomach."

Yeshua rolled over and his friend started massaging his neck and upper back. "Listen, Jew, that Library will kill you."

"How is Jasmine?"

"Fine. I am seeing her more often. Thank you for the marvelous evening at her home."

"I am sure the marvelous part was due to her, not you or me."

"I will not argue."

"Good, you would lose."

"Listen, we are finished for today. Join us for some falafel and wine."

"All right. Fine."

Three of them and Yeshua made their way to a small place on the river. Not a restaurant, a place for appetizers and wine. They took a table on the water. Farad ordered. The river slithered by, a long green eel shimmering in afternoon sun. A waiter placed a plate of small fried fish and falafel, a decanter of wine and cups before them. Farad uttered a brief Persian blessing and they began.

Yeshua said, "These fish are wonderful. What are they?"

One of the others answered. "Pilchard."

Afterwards, Farad and Yeshua walked along the shore. "How much longer will you stay with us, Hebrew?"

"Several more months, at least."

"Stay. We all love you. As I said the other night, you are like a Persian. We will find you a fine Persian woman."

"Jasmine is the only one I would want."

"You would have to fight me for her."

"I would lose, and happy to lose. She belongs with you."

Farad laughed, grabbed him around the neck and bumped his friend's chest with his fist.

"Yeshua, my place is this direction. Good evening."

"Be safe."

Yeshua spent one afternoon in the Library, one in the gymnasium. His physical toughness came back. One afternoon, he stopped at the market for vegetables. There were Farad and Jasmine. "Farad! I see you stole my girlfriend."

"Bah! Hebrew, you do not have a chance."

All three looked over the stalls. Each gathering what they wanted.

Yeshua said, "Good to see you, my friends. I must go."

Jasmine said, "Wait, Librarian. I will walk with you." They started away.

Farad spoke up. "Yeshua, I hate you!"

"Makes me happy."

They walked. Jasmine said, "I love the way you two friends play. You disguise your affectation for one another."

"You do not mind we use you as a pawn?"

"Not at all. What woman would not like two fine men pretending to compete for her?"

"Who says we are pretending?"

"Oh stop, Yeshua! Do not treat me like a dull person. I know there is a woman waiting for you in Palestine."

"Actually no, ... Alexandria."

"Aha! She must be beautiful."

"In many ways, as you are beautiful in many ways, some different than her."

"You are such a flatterer."

"Not at all. I do not flatter. What I said was the truth. You and Farad are Persian. Esther and I are Hebrew. That is the way it is."

"And you just accept things ... the way they are."

"I accept God's ways, and I decide what I must do every day. The trick is the balance. Or ... perhaps it is doing what I do while staying in touch with God."

"You can manage that?"

"I am not sure. Why do you think I have my nose in those scrolls all the time?"

"Is it necessary?"

"I begin to believe it is not."

"Here is my home. Goodbye, my good friend."

"Shalom, my fine friend."

In the evening Melchior asked, "What are you studying now?"

"Buddhism. I am intrigued. It seems a balanced approach. Wisdom, conduct, then mind and spirit. But ignoring the place of God in our lives does not make sense to me."

"I believe our marvelous world had to be created. This means a creator is behind it. We see the creator all around us, in the circumstances of life, in nature and in our hearts. God's *invisible attributes, His eternal power and divine nature have been clearly perceived since the creation of the world in the things that have been made.* At times *we see through a glass dimly*, but we do see if we wish to."

Reza was quiet these days. One morning he said, "Yeshua, I am not going back. I have accepted a position here."

"I sensed that. But Babylon is unstable. Two hundred years ago it dwindled in size after Alexander's followers fought over it. It has grown back, but there are always warring factions. Alexandria is much more solid."

"I know, but this is my home."

"I understand being away from home."

Yeshua moved on, studying Taoism. This religion emerged about four hundred years earlier in China. Central to its teachings was living in harmony with the universe and its pattern. Drawing on the precepts of Lao-Tse, it emphasized spontaneity and effortless action. It disdained ritual practices, concentrating on living the faith. Like many other religions and philosophies, it discouraged craving and desires. It was about contentment.

One month later on the veranda Yeshua said, "I am leaving."

Aliyah's eyes misted. Melchior said, "Well, we all knew this day would come. When?"

"Soon."

Yeshua arranged to join a caravan heading northeast where he could transfer to another one headed for Palestine. The evening before departure, Mahan, his wife, Jasmine and Farad came to the home for evening meal. They spoke little.

After eating, they all stood on the veranda sipping Shiraz, early fall breezes caressing their faces. Mahan approached. "We will miss you, young man."

"Thank you for everything, sir."

His wife came, giving her goodbyes and blessings.

Next was Jasmine. After she hugged him, he said, "Goodbye, lovely one. Perhaps in another life." She turned and looked down.

Farad approached. Yeshua reached out to his shoulder and guided him away. "Listen my friend. Things are uncertain here. If it gets bad again, come to Alexandria. The city is prosperous and tolerant. Greeks, Jews, Egyptians, other foreigners. I have many friends and connections. The Library will always know where I am."

"You know I will never leave."

"Would you endanger her?"

Farad pursed his lips. "Goodbye, my brother. I will not forget you."

"Shalom."

They clutched each other hard. Across the room Jasmine watched, eyes blinking.

Before dawn the next morning, Yeshua, Aliyah and Melchior walked up the Processional Way toward the Ishtar Gate, built six centuries earlier at the direction of King Nebuchadnezzar II. Both the Gate and the Way were deep blue in color imitating the Lapis Lazuli stone, prized for jewelry throughout the Middle East and beyond. Images of animals representing three Persian gods lined the Way and the Gate. Dragons depicted

Marduk, head of the gods. The bull represented Adad, also one of the chief gods. Adad's province was the weather. The goddess Ishtar gave her name to the Gate. The lion was her symbol and she represented sexuality.

They walked through the gate and came to Yeshua's caravan, preparing to depart. Aliyah grabbed Yeshua, crying as she held him. "You have brought us much joy these past months. You are the son I never had." She let go, pushed away and stood holding her face.

Melchior embraced the person he visited so long ago as a child. "You came as far to see us as I once came to see you, even farther. Since the day you walked into my office, my life has reached its fulfillment. Now I will watch the sunset, gazing at my cherished stars, knowing somewhere you look at the same sky, and I will think of you and pray for you."

Yeshua said, "As I watch the same sky, I will thank God you found me long ago, and now I found you. God bless you for everything." He gave the old man a long hug. Then he found his camel, climbed on and urged it up. He spun the animal and stood looking at them until the caravan started moving. He raised his hand.

They blew kisses at him as he rode away. Aliyah said, "We will never see him again."

"We will always have him in our hearts and minds, and he will have us. Be thankful for these past precious months." They watched until the long line of camels disappeared over the hill, then they turned and walked back to their home.

The caravan began its long arc north and west up the great rivers until it reached Al Bukamal. There Yeshua switched caravans for the hot trek across the desert to Palestine. Just past the Golan Heights as they reached the Sea of Galilee, he left the group and headed for Nazareth. Arriving at Mary's home, several of the boys saw him.

They screamed, "Mother! It is Yeshua!" He settled his mount as Mary sprang from the house, looking as she always did, ... ageless.

"Son!" She ran toward him, and they clung to each other as he lifted her off the ground. All the children jumped and grabbed him. He looked at the tallest.

"James, is that you? You are as big as I am! Here, camel-driver, take care of this animal. I am tired."

Mary said, "Children, bring the table and chairs outside. It is a good night and we still have some light." Soon, pieces of furniture faced down the hill to Sepphoris.

His mother asked, "Are you hungry, son?"

"Yes."

"Perfect. We are about to eat. Children, bring the food."

The little army surged into the house. Food was piled on the table, and the two daughters dispensed it to plates, then handed them to Mary, Yeshua, then the rest.

As he received his plate he said, "Rachel, you are still the tallest, but I cannot tell if you or Leah is the most beautiful." Rachel kissed him on the cheek. Nearby Leah just smiled.

The next morning as he sat drinking tea, looking toward Sepphoris, Simon came and joined him. "Brother, you always approach from the south. Last night you came from the north."

"You have a good eye."

"Well?"

"I came from Babylon. I was there many months."

"Babylon! For what purpose?"

"I learned about the people, I made friends, I studied their religion and their ways, I studied other religions."

"But you are Hebrew!"

"And I will always be Hebrew. We have a great revelation of God. Simon, ... *This is the work of God, ... that you **believe**.* Our God is not small. We make Him small. God and the world are large, and beautiful people fill the world."

Yeshua stood. "I go to see Grandfather. Would you like to come?"

"Yes!"

"Saddle the camel. You drive."

He ran.

Yeshua walked to the house and entered. Mary was at the window, looking out. "Mother, I go to see Grandfather. I will take Simon." She nodded. He grabbed an orange and a piece of bread and walked out.

Simon guided the animal down the slope. They neared their grandparents' home, and he put the camel down. Yeshua jumped off and walked to the door. Anna saw him and screamed. She ran. Joachim was close behind.

"Son, we have not heard from you. We worried."

Anna asked, "Some tea?"

"Sure."

"Are you hungry?"

"No. Simon may be." They went inside.

He spent a week at home, then traveled to Caesarea Maritima and caught a ship for Alexandria. The day after docking, Esther emerged from the synagogue as school ended. A very dark, sunburnt man stood watching her. He was dressed in colorful Persian clothes and boots, a white covering wrapped around his head and neck. She glanced at him, then walked away. She stopped and looked sideways. A brilliant white line of teeth split the brown face and he spread his arms.

"Yeshua!" She ran to him. They embraced a long time.

"Are you going to market?"

"With a Persian? Certainly not!"

She grabbed his arm. "You may escort me home, Persian, but I am not sure I trust you."

"Might be wise. Persians have different ways."

"No joking now. Why did you stay so long?"

"I found Melchior and stayed with him and his wife. They were wonderful. I studied eastern religions. I made good friends."

"Female friends?"

"One. My best friend's woman."

"Why did you not steal her and bring her back?"

"I could not get you out of my heart and mind."

Esther pulled his arm lower and kissed his cheek.

They arrived at her home. "Come in, my parents will be thrilled to see you."

"Soon enough. I will walk alone and get reacquainted with the city."

"Change your clothing first. Shalom."

"As the Arabs say, Salaam alaikum."

The Jewish Quarter was in the far northeast of the city. Yeshua walked south along the city wall. He came to the Canopic Gate. The Canopic Way split the city in half right through its central district, beginning at the Western or Moon Gate and ending at the Canopic Gate in the east. He passed on, continuing south then turning west as the walls veered in that direction. He passed the Solis Gate; its avenue split the city north to south, intersecting the Canopic Way and forming a great cross. Beyond this southern wall lay the Alexandrian canal, sometimes called the Nile canal, cut from the western-most tributary of the Nile delta. Continuing on he came to the Serapeum, site of a Greek temple built three hundred years earlier. Past there the wall moved north, and reaching the Western Moon Gate, Yeshua turned east and strolled the Canopic Way through the heart of the city, passing three Greco-Egyptian temples, then bypassing the harbor he knew so well and headed northeast past his beloved gymnasium and Library, and ended again in the Jewish Quarter in the northeast.

It was dark when he knocked on the door. Yari opened it. "We wondered where you were!"

"I needed to walk."

"Come. Get something to eat." They sat in the kitchen. Fish, vegetables, rice, white wine. "You are so dark, I almost did not see you outside."

"That will fade with Library work."

Yeshua and Philo fell into their work together. After a week, the older man said, "I missed you. It is so enjoyable to work with you again. Were you surprised when Reza stayed in Babylon?"

"No."

Several months went by. One day around noon Philo said, "Let us get some food."

"Sure."

As they ate at their place on the harbor, Philo said, "The authorities want me to visit Rome."

"For what purpose?"

"Agitation between the Greeks and the Jews. It is becoming worse. I am seen as a bridge between the two cultures."

"This is accurate. Perhaps you can do some good."

"I want you to come with me. You have broad experience. Raised in Palestine; you have lived in Persia and here in Egypt. You move easily between cultures. You would be a great help to me, and it would advance your reputation."

"You know I do not care about that."

"You are too idealistic."

"Perhaps. But, I will come."

"Thank you."

Within two weeks they were on a ship bound for Italy. They landed at Brindisi on the bottom of the Italian boot. From there they traveled overland to Rome. Up the arid heel of Italy, through the Saracen-Arab type dwellings, heading north.

Approaching Rome from the east, they saw the above-ground portion of the Aqua Appia aqueduct. Philo asked, "What do you think, craftsman?"

"Impressive."

"Who would think to build such a structure to carry water?"

Yeshua replied, "The Persians."

"Not the Romans?"

"The Romans do not invent much of anything. Their architecture, their sculpture, their philosophy, even their religion is borrowed from the Greeks and others. Roman genius lies in engineering, building, organization, and always improvement. But I never saw anything this grand in Persia."

Rome

The Roman Forum was the center of the city. They found lodgings in the small Jewish quarter. It was comfortable for them. They had a few days before the meetings began.

They roamed the Forum, awestruck. Philo said, "The roofs on some of these temples are massive, much larger than in Greece or Alexandria."

Yeshua said, "Look how almost every temple has walls behind the front and side columns. This supports greater weight than just using Greek columns. All these temples were rebuilt over the centuries, made stronger, more modern. The Temples of Vesta, Jupiter, Apollo. The Roman mastery of concrete in building allows much more construction with far less expense than strictly marble."

They walked to the Circus Maximus, the site of the famous chariot races. The entire complex measured 600 meters in length and over 100 meters in width. There was room for 150,000 spectators. Philo let out a low whistle. "I see what you mean about using concrete."

Yeshua said, "There are at least two other Circuses. This is the largest. They are not only used for chariot races, also gladiatorial contests, festivals and so on."

As the day faded they returned near the Jewish quarter, found a simple *trattoria,* ordered and enjoyed the dying sunlight. "Yeshua, tomorrow we begin the discussions in the Basilica Aemilia in the Forum."

"What do you expect?"

"I expect rowdiness. These are passionate, intelligent groups of people, as you and I well know. Greeks and Jews."

"How will you approach things?"

"Let them exhaust themselves to some degree, let the energy subside. Then we look for common ground, some give and take, identify the leaders, try to appeal to reason."

"Will not the leaders be obvious?"

"No. There will be a spokesperson for each body, but there will also be one or two influential people in the group. Try to discern who they are."

"How?"

"Use that intuition of yours."

"You expect success?"

"Yeshua, this is not about outright success or failure. Think about partial success or partial failure. It is my job as negotiator to try and tip the scales to partial success. Please share any insights with me. Do not hold back."

The next morning they walked to the Forum and found the Basilica or meeting place where official gatherings took place. Again, Philo was impressed. "Three stories, Yeshua, and just as you said, concrete walls in the rear of the structure supporting the upper floors. Simple, yet ingenious."

They entered and asked directions to the meeting.

The meeting room was large, bright and airy. A long table, opposing sides facing one another. Philo and Yeshua took seats at one end. Two Romans sat at the other end. Down the long sides, the combatants stared across at each other.

The Romans at the far end stood and introduced themselves. The chief spokesman for each side was asked to briefly state his argument. The Greek spokesman stood and stated the Jewish contingent (and others in their community) criticized Greek philosophy and beliefs in belittling terms. The Greeks also claimed the Jews extended their animosity to obstructing Greek businesses by undercutting prices.

The Jewish spokesman countered that the Greeks were intolerant of non-Greeks, in particular Jewish merchants and others who refused to worship Greek gods.

Accusations flew back and forth across the table. To their credit, the Roman moderators managed to keep interruptions to a minimum, allowing both sides to have a reasonable amount of time to air differences.

Yeshua watched closely, leaned to Philo and pointed out another Greek near the spokesman. After half an hour, one of the Roman "referees" stood, motioned for silence and introduced Philo and Yeshua. Philo was described as a "Greek Jew" and a leading scholar at the Library of Alexandria. Yeshua was introduced as a Palestinian Jew, who had studied at Alexandria for years in addition to Babylon, had many Greek colleagues, and was fluent in Greek, various dialects of Aramaic, including Persian.

Philo stood and began, speaking in Greek. "Gentlemen, your arguments fall into two clear categories, religious and mercantile. My question is quite simple, I ask your response be simple. Which is the more important issue? Religion or business?" Philo nodded to the Greek spokesman.

The Greek leaned over and spoke to several of his companions, including the man Yeshua had pointed out. Then he stood and said, "Religious. Do not denigrate our gods."

Philo then nodded at the Jewish spokesman. He rose. "Both are important, but I must agree. Religious respect is the more important."

Philo said, "I know of no one who has more respect for other religions than my colleague. I would like him to say a few words."

Yeshua rose. "Gentlemen, I am from Palestine, I love my faith, but I respect other religions. I suggest we realize we all have different revelations of God, but we are all brothers."

The man who the Greek spokesman had privately conversed with said, "Just a moment, Hebrew. Philo said you lived in Babylon. I am a Persian-Greek from Babylon. What did you do there?"

"I worked at the Library."

"Ah. You worked at the Great Library. Who did you work with?"

"Melchior, the astrologer. He is an old friend. I lived in his home. I also am friends with Mahan, the Head Librarian. I have been in his home many times."

The man's smugness faded. "You know Mahan and his family. What is his daughter's name?"

"Jasmine."

A tight grin appeared on the man's face. "Salaam alaikum."

"Alaikum el Salaam."

The Persian-Greek leaned toward his spokesman and whispered a few words.

After some discussion both sides agreed to respect each other's religious views and not to meddle in the other's business dealings.

The Greek leader rose. "We are satisfied."

Philo looked to the Jewish spokesman.

"We are satisfied also."

The meeting was over.

Yeshua approached the Persian-Greek, speaking in Babylonian dialect.

The Persian leaned toward Yeshua. "I thought you were lying."

"Of course you did. I would have thought the same. When you are in Babylon again, please give my best wishes to Melchior and Mahan."

"I will." They parted company.

Yeshua said, "Philo, perhaps it went better than you thought."

"It is but a partial success. There will still be incidents. Hopefully fewer."

The next day they visited the Library built by Caesar Augustus. It adjoined the Temple of Apollo Palatinus. It was vast. They looked over available manuscripts. "There is not much here, Yeshua, and I doubt we will be fortunate to acquire anything worthwhile. They know who I am, and they have seen you with me. Let us just browse our own interests. How is an hour?"

"Fine."

Within two days they were at Ostia Antica, the port of Rome, ready to board a ship bound for Alexandria.

*****

Today, Rome is a beehive of activity. If you walk south down the great Corso, the main boulevard in center city, you come to the monument of Victor Emmanuel II. Just past it you may climb as I did to the Piazza del Campidoglio overlooking the ancient Roman Forum.

The Forum is littered with the fallen pieces of history. The pavement is from Augustus, transporting us back in time two thousand years to when Yeshua and Philo strolled the very same way. At twilight the ghosts of Rome's past weave through those stones and the few remaining columns, remembering a glorious history, sensing a sensual present, and dreaming of a future stretching to eternity.

Eternal Rome. *"Non basta, una vita."* One life is not enough.

Syracuse

The voyage to Alexandria was rough. The autumn north winds drove the vessel hard through churning waves. Philo remained below. Yeshua braved the upper deck, feeling the force of Nature and God, showing us we are not really in control, though we are often tempted to believe so.

The ship clung to the west coast of Italy, making for the straits of Messina where Sicily almost touched the mainland. They surged through the passage, down the east coast of Sicily. The vicious north wind returned. The ship hugged the coast. Yeshua made his way to the rear of the ship where the captain stood with his steersman.

"What will you do?"

"We will put in at Syracuse. This is too much. Go below."

Yeshua made his way back to the cabin.

The ship continued south through the night. Though winds were fierce, the sky was clear, and the moon and stars gave enough light to allow progress. As dawn broke they neared Syracuse. The northern small port was not appropriate. It faced northeast into the winds. The captain guided them south around the island of Ortygia, barely separated from the mainland. Shaped like a large hand with a jagged forefinger pointing south, it held the chief portion of the city. They skirted around the thin peninsula and turned north into the sheltered harbor. Shielded from the wind, the ship docked.

Philo was terribly seasick. "Son, how long will we be here?"

"I do not know."

"Find out. If it is any decent length of time, I must get off the boat."

Yeshua left and was soon back. "Probably several days."

"Let us find an inn."

They made their way topside, and Yeshua spoke with the captain. "Let us know where you stay. We will not leave without you."

They made their way ashore and found the first decent inn. He got Philo into bed.

"You need something to eat."

"I cannot eat."

"You must. You have been vomiting. At least some soup."

"All right."

Yeshua left and went to the kitchen. "I need soup. Good quantity, thin."

"I have an onion soup."

"Fine."

He returned with a large vessel. "Sit up. Here is a spoon. Take your time, but keep putting it down."

Philo nodded. Yeshua walked back to the dining area and sat. A young woman approached. "May I help you?"

"Tea to start with, please."

She soon came back with a pot, some sugar and lemon wedges. "Thank you."

He gazed out the window at the port, wind howling. The boats bounced high, water washing up on the wharf. The tea was good and strong. The girl returned. "Would you like some breakfast?"

"Yes. Eggs, bread, cheese, tomatoes, if you are able to do that."

"Of course. You have a good appetite for just coming off a rough ship."

"I am blessed with a good stomach."

In a short time she approached with the food. "Here you are, Hebrew."

"Is it so obvious?"

"For us of the same faith, yes. My father and I see many types of people here."

"You and your father operate this place?"

"Yes. May I sit down?"

"Of course."

Yeshua ate earnestly. The young lady was amused. "You must be a sailor."

"No, I am far from a sailor."

"What then?"

"A bit of a scholar. I work at the Library of Alexandria."

"If you work there, you must be more than a 'bit' of a scholar."

An older man approached. "Hannah, who is this?"

"He is one of us, Father. He is from Alexandria."

Yeshua rose. "Please join us, sir."

He sat. "What are you doing here?"

"Our ship is delayed by the winds. My companion is in our room, very seasick."

"I lived in Alexandria for many years. I do not recognize you or your accent. Who is your companion?"

"Philo of the Library."

"You work with him?"

"I do."

Some other customers entered. Hannah went to take their order.

Yeshua asked, "What made you come here from Alexandria?"

"There was an opportunity. I have friends here. For the past 200 years, Roman rule made it stable."

Yeshua rose. "Good speaking with you. I should check on Philo. Shalom."

"Shalom."

He entered the room. Philo sat up in the bed. The bowl was empty. "You finished the soup."

"Yes, without incident."

"How do you feel?"

"Better. The dizziness is gone, the stomach settled. Still weak."

"Well, relax. With this wind I doubt we are going anywhere."

While Philo recovered, Yeshua roamed around the "Windy City." Syracuse was the capital of Sicily, a Greek/Roman metropolis as Sicily was once part of *Magna Graecia* (Greater Greece) before Roman rule. Theocritus the poet and Plato the philosopher spent time in Syracuse. Archimedes the great Greek geometrician was born, lived and died here.

He passed the Temple of Apollo, an early Doric-styled structure. To the northeast was the Euryalas fortress, built hundreds of years earlier for defense because of its high strategic location. Much used because Syracuse went through numerous sieges by Carthage and others (and many changes of rulers) until Rome brought order. At this time it rivaled Athens in size and strength as a "Greek" capital. In the west sat the Temple of the Olympian Zeus, the second oldest monument after Apollo's and also Doric in design. Appropriate for the sea-faring Greeks, it gazed out to the sea from higher ground to the entrance of the harbor.

Within two days Philo was moving. Hannah and her father made sure he was looked after. After three days the wind lessened. On the fourth day the ship captain visited the inn. Yeshua drank tea with Hannah's father.

"Join us, Captain."

"Thank you, no. I have other stops to make. How is Philo?"

"Much better."

"Good. If the wind continues to weaken, we may depart in one or two days. I will know when is our best chance."

"Chance?"

"Well, I am not Poseidon, but I have a good nose for these things. I will call early one of these mornings. Be ready to move quickly."

"All right, Captain." He left.

In two days, the captain knocked at their door at dawn. Yeshua opened it.

"We cast off."

"Philo is ready. We come right away."

"Good."

They grabbed their bags and headed to the ship. The breeze was firm. Soon the captain boarded and other passengers followed. Philo went below. Mooring ropes were cast off. The ship edged away from the dock. It veered to the harbor entrance and disappeared into the sea.

*****

My last view of Syracuse was from the highway south of the Temple of the Olympian Zeus. A sunny, Sicilian afternoon. The island of Ortygia with its central hill and long peninsular neck pointing south was a dazzling white swan resting in the water near the mainland.

*****

They sailed southeast with a good breeze, reached the coast of North Africa, then hugged the coast, moving east. Near sunset the second day, the great shining Pharos split the sky. They were home.

The next afternoon, he was outside the synagogue school at dismissal.

"Esther, something to eat?"

"Of course, I must tell my parents. They will worry."

They walked to her home, she went in for a few minutes then returned.

They found a restaurant on the water, ordered and sat. Silence.

"What is it, Yeshua?"

"I am finished with travel."

Her face lit up. "Wonderful! What about Palestine?"

"The only exception. I have seen the world. It has nothing more for me. In essence people are much the same everywhere. Some cultural differences."

"Alexandria is a wonderful place. It is as good as any."

"It is better. You are here."

She reached over and placed her hand on top of his.

The next morning Yeshua sat with Philo looking over manuscripts. Philo said, "Reza is gone, but the arrangement remains. Half day with me, afternoons free. What adventure will you pursue next?"

"I am going back to our writings, the Hebrew scriptures."

"Which part?"

"The Psalms. I am of the House of David. His passionate heart craved God and could not stand any absence. His psalms are lyrical, and I love music. I adore his use of metaphor. Some day I will teach in a similar way. It resonates with people, not the dry repetition. You also have helped me with this, with your mastery of allegory."

"You are kind."

"People often accuse me of kindness. I am truthful."

"You are both."

He began to take a more active part in the synagogue, reading aloud. In time he added a bit of commentary. He grew less talkative, more contented. Esther noticed and mentioned it.

"I feel God's presence more and more, Esther."

"The Psalms?"

"They help, but it is more. I do a great amount of thinking, which of course, you know. Most of our thinking is about the past and the future. When I simply sense the present, I am more at peace. I begin to believe this is what God meant in our scriptures when He said His true name is 'I Am.'"

"You believe it is so simple?"

"That simple, that profound, that unusual. If faith, believing and trusting are so important, how can we do those things when we worry about the future or relive the past?"

"So we should think about the present."

"Not exactly. I believe we should *experience* the present moment, live in it, not think about it. I believe that is the true meaning of "I Am."

She said, "But we must learn from the past and plan for the future."

"Of course we must. The problem is not in learning or planning. Those are natural and good. The problem is not in learning from the past, but in rethinking those lessons, then thinking again, over and over. The problem lies not in planning for the future, but in replanning, then going over it in our minds again and again. Over-thinking is the same as worry. Worry is not faith, it is not trust, it is not believing, ... it is just obsessive thinking. I believe God will guide us if we just allow Him. If we stay with 'I Am.' *With God, all things are possible."*

"Yeshua, you are basing a great deal on 'I Am.'"

"It is repeated over and over, for example when our Scriptures state, *'Be still, and know that I Am God.'* Is this not saying the same thing? How about in the book of Micah when it says, *'What does the Lord require of you but to do justice, to love kindness and walk humbly with your God.'* All three of those actions take place Now, in the 'I Am.' Do not walk in *your past,* do not walk in *your future,* ... *walk humbly with God Now."*

"It sounds peaceful."

"It is. Bitterness, anger and resentment come from *the past.* Worry, fear and anxiety come from *the future.* Who would want to be trapped in those prisons? But we place ourselves there. Walking with the great 'I Am,' ... *Now* is peaceful."

"Why are we not taught this in synagogue?"

"A synagogue is a place of learning, and we Hebrews above all, are people of the Book. We revere learning and the mind. *We search the Scriptures because in them we think we have Life."*

"Yeshua, you above all have been a man of learning, a man of books."

"Yes, I believed it was the correct way. Now I see it is helpful, but not sufficient. We must go beyond our foundations. We must find the 'I Am' who is beyond words. The One the Greeks call the *Logos*, the unspoken *Word*. The Hindus refer to *'AUM.'* Even here in Egypt is the idea of an omnipresent God. And I must seek to walk with Him. We should all seek that. He is not only present; He is *active.*"

"You sound very hungry."

"And thirsty. There is a wonderful passage in my beloved Psalms, which speaks of this. Ironically, it is not a psalm of David, although it could be. *'As a deer pants for flowing streams, so my soul pants for you, O God. My soul pants for God, for the living God. When shall I come and appear before God.'*"

"It is beautiful."

"Notice how it speaks of the 'living God,' the God of *Now.*"

"What I believe ... is the local rabbi should protect his job."

He chuckled. "Esther, you bring me back to earth. The local rabbi's job is secure. And it is a lovely sunset." After a few more minutes, he said, "Come, I must get you home. It is not proper for a good Hebrew woman to be out after dark, especially with a man rumored to be Persian."

"I hear there are some fine Persians."

"You are correct. I have some dear friends there."

They walked toward the Jewish quarter in the twilight. She clung to him a little more closely than usual. "Persian, thank you for sharing your heart to me tonight."

"My heart is always open to you."

"Yes, but tonight you shared deeply. I enjoyed it."

They came to her home. He grabbed both her shoulders and kissed her lightly on the forehead.

She said, "I must say knowing you for years now, a kiss on the cheek, the eyes, the forehead, is quite frustrating."

"It is frustrating for me also."

"Well, I guess that is some comfort."

There was a long embrace. He kissed her on the other side of the forehead.

"Shalom, Persian.

"Shalom."

Yeshua took to walking with her to the synagogue in the morning before he went to the Library.

One morning she said, "Yeshua, most of the people I know are good, yet I also know there is much wrong in the world. Why?"

"I do not know, but I know in our scriptures it says, *'God created man upright, but he sought out many devices.'* I also know *it is the Spirit that gives Life, the flesh profits nothing. The words God speaks to us, they are Spirit and they are Life."* We must listen for His voice."

Yeshua worked at the Library, exercised at the gymnasium, served at synagogue, attended his aunt and uncle's parties, but something was itching him.

One night after a very nice evening in Yari and Miriam's home, Esther and Yeshua walked back toward her house. "Esther, I am leaving tomorrow."

"Another of your annual trips?"

"No. I will not be back in a month."

"When?"

"I do not know."

"Yeshua, I am very tired of being a "respectable" young Hebrew woman. I am tired of not asserting myself, waiting for my indecisive friend to make a decision."

"I am very decisive about many things."

"Not the important things."

"Here is a bench. Let us sit." They sat. "I feel drawn to Palestine. I believe God has something very important for me there."

"What? Synagogue work? You could be the head rabbi in any synagogue here or there!"

"No. There is a man in Galilee who ministers to people in the countryside. He speaks the Word of God without restriction, with freedom. Actually he is a relative, although that is not important."

"So, you want to become one of his disciples?"

"No, I believe differently than he, but I want to have a similar ministry."

"To what end?"

"Esther, Palestine is suffering. Between the Romans and the chief priests, they strangle the people."

"Palestine is always suffering. What do you think you can accomplish?"

"I do not know, but I must try."

"What about me?"

"What about you?"

Esther threw up her hands. "Men! It is always about ... you!"

"Perhaps you are correct there."

"There is no 'perhaps' ... Yeshua, take me with you."

"No. It is not like here. It is rough, and it is dangerous. It might be dangerous for me, and it would be for my woman."

"I am not afraid."

"I am. I will not endanger you."

"Yeshua, I am tired mincing words. I love you. Do you love me?"

"No."

Her face moved up and back. She stared at him.

"Esther, I do not love you. Love is a weak term. The Greeks have four different words for it. I do not love you. I adore you. Since the first night in that garden. It has not changed, except grown deeper."

"So there is no secret woman in Palestine?"

Yeshua threw back his head and laughed. "You know better."

"I am coming with you to Palestine."

"No, you are not."

Her face grew hard and red. "Yeshua of Nazareth, you are the most infuriating man in the world. I love you, ... and I hate you! Goodbye!"

She marched to her house, walked in and slammed the door.

Yari, Miriam and Yeshua stood on the dock the next morning, the ship bound for Palestine in front of them. Miriam was crying. Even her husband had a tear in his eye.

Yari said, "Son, remember. If this does not work out, you always have a home here."

He nodded.

Miriam grabbed and kissed him. "We love you."

"I have never doubted it."

Suddenly, Esther appeared at Miriam's side ... Silence.

Yeshua looked at her, then walked toward the ship. As he was about to step onto the gangplank, Esther screamed, "Yeshua!" He turned as she ran and leaped into his arms, her eyes streaming. He held her off the ground for a long moment, then kissed each of her eyelids.

"Yeshua, you magnificent fool. Come back to me!"

He picked up his bag and walked onto the ship, moving forward as he always did. Esther returned to Miriam's side. The boat began moving. The women waved. As usual, they watched until the craft turned to sea and they lost his face.

He went back to Nazareth and reacquainted himself with the area and the people, dividing his time between Nazareth, Sepphoris and Capernaum. He spent time in "the wilderness" around "the Baptist."

We all know the rest of the story.

Jesus of Nazareth began a three-year nomadic ministry in Palestine. He sometimes read and spoke in his home synagogue in Nazareth, although they did not like some of the things he said, and they even seemed a bit uncertain of his exact identity or perhaps they could not believe a local village man would be so eloquent and stunning. He had only lived one month a year in the region for the past ten years, sometimes less. He spent time at his family's second home in Capernaum on the Sea of Galilee. He spoke in the synagogue there and attracted crowds in the countryside. He recruited followers (disciples), performed miracles and exorcisms and began speaking to larger and larger crowds. He was way beyond compelling ... it was magnetic ... *electrifying.* He did not simply recite texts as most rabbis did. Like David he used his beloved metaphors. But he used them to convey heavenly lessons in an earthly way, ... parables. It was not religious ... it was *Spiritual.* He spent a considerable period of time in the Galilee and Jordan River areas. His reputation mushroomed. Then he and his band began traveling in a great arc to Jerusalem, where the ultimate confrontation came. A collision course. The Jewish authorities in Jerusalem condemned him. They saw him as a religious threat. He challenged their power and authority.

The Roman officials were always on the lookout for rebellion (there was plenty of it). They also condemned him. He was crucified with two other trouble-makers.

His death on the cross is quite mystifying. Although young and strong, he did not last long at all. True, he had gone through quite an ordeal at his trial. But in a short time he appeared limp and dead. Most crucifixions last a very long time, victims struggling to push themselves up, gasping for breath, as the weight of their bodies on the cross makes it impossible to breathe. The slow suffocation of crucifixion is a horrible way to die.

Often the authorities broke the leg bones of those on the cross so they could not push up for breath. This quickened the end. Jesus quickly appeared quite dead without struggle, so they did not break his legs. One of the guards plunged a spear into his side.

Joseph of Arimathea, a member of the religious hierarchy, and a secret admirer of Jesus, asked Pontius Pilate for the body, which was granted. Joseph and Nicodemus, another religious leader, also a secret friend, retrieved the body, bound and laid it in a tomb owned by Joseph.

The next morning both male and female followers of Jesus visited the tomb. It was empty. There are various accounts of Jesus appearing to his followers over the next forty days.

*****

Two months after the crucifixion, at Caesarea Maritima a tall well-built man, perhaps thirty years of age, boarded a boat bound for Alexandria. He moved with a calm presence, as if unaware of all the ship activity around him. He seemed from a different time, a different place. Walking to the front of the craft, the man grabbed the rigging, and as they turned to the sea he smiled into the morning sun, long dark hair rippling in the wind.

Beneath flowing robes there was a large scar on his side.

About the Author

Dr. David Lundberg holds degrees from the United States Air Force Academy, Boston University and the University of North Carolina. He and his wife try to divide their time between America and Europe.

Made in the USA
Columbia, SC
12 March 2021